"What are you doing here?" Adam demanded.

"I'm looking for you." Christy walked into Adam's office and taking a deep breath for courage, said, "Will you kiss me?"

"I don't think that would be a good idea," Adam said, his voice brusque.

"Why not?" Christy smiled wryly. "I like you, Adam, and I think you like me. Would it be so wrong for us to get to know each other?"

"Yes, it would be wrong," he responded firmly. "I don't have time for you in my life right now. Hell, I don't even have time to sleep."

"Kiss me, Adam. Prove to me that you know how to live. Show me that you have hot blood running through your veins instead of ledgers and letterheads."

Adam was furious. Christy made him sound as if he were a machine. He pulled her onto his lap and brushed his lips over hers, reveling at her sigh. For once "Christmas" might be worth looking forward to....

For **Carin Rafferty**, Christmas is a time for renewing her faith in the innate goodness of mankind and the innocence of childhood. The idea for *Christmas Knight* came from a letter a seven-year-old boy wrote to Santa Claus—all he wanted for Christmas was for his parents to stop fighting so his father could come home and they could be a family. Carin's heart went out to him, and she wondered how his attitude toward Christmas would change if Santa Claus didn't make that wish come true. From that question, *Christmas Knight* evolved into a delightfully heartwarming and humorous Christmas tale.

Look for Carin's *The Hood* in February— the second romance in REBELS AND ROGUES, our celebration of the hero.

Books by Carin Rafferty

HARLEQUIN TEMPTATION
319–MY FAIR BABY
363–SHERLOCK AND WATSON

Don't miss any of our special offers. Write to us at the following address for information on our newest releases.

Harlequin Reader Service
P.O. Box 1397, Buffalo, NY 14240
Canadian address: P.O. Box 603,
Fort Erie, Ont. L2A 5X3

Christmas Knight
CARIN RAFFERTY

Harlequin Books

TORONTO • NEW YORK • LONDON
AMSTERDAM • PARIS • SYDNEY • HAMBURG
STOCKHOLM • ATHENS • TOKYO • MILAN

With love to my family and friends,
and a special season's greeting to all my loyal readers

Published December 1991

ISBN 0-373-25473-3

CHRISTMAS KNIGHT

Copyright © 1991 by Linda Kichline. All rights reserved.
Except for use in any review, the reproduction or utilization
of this work in whole or in part in any form by any electronic,
mechanical or other means, now known or hereafter invented,
including xerography, photocopying and recording,
or in any information storage or retrieval system, is forbidden without
the permission of the publisher, Harlequin Enterprises Limited,
225 Duncan Mill Road, Don Mills, Ontario, Canada M3B 3K9.

All the characters in this book have no existence outside the
imagination of the author and have no relation whatsoever to
anyone bearing the same name or names. They are not even
distantly inspired by any individual known or unknown to the
author, and all incidents are pure invention.

® are Trademarks registered in the United States Patent and
Trademark Office and in other countries.

Printed in U.S.A.

1

ADAM WORTH DUCKED his head and raced across Evergreen Mall's parking lot. Buffeted by the strong, bitterly cold wind, he held the collar of his topcoat closed with one hand and tried to control its flapping hem with the other. According to the weatherman, this wind was a harbinger of a major winter snowstorm for Colorado Springs, Colorado. Adam prayed that the weatherman was wrong, but the way his luck was running, he not only expected a major storm, but a hundred-year-record breaker.

Why in the world had he set a holiday-season opening date for the mall? he asked himself while sliding his key into the lock of the main entrance. As a child, he'd watched Christmas approach with the same exuberance as a prisoner on death row. Now, he considered it a hectic business season with more headaches than it was worth. Despite his aversion to the holidays, he knew that December was the best retail month of the year and that Evergreen Mall, located as it was on *Evergreen* Road, would appeal to the whimsical spirit of holiday shoppers. It was a marketing dream come true, and he couldn't have ignored it even if he'd wanted to.

He opened the door a crack, slipped inside and locked it. Then he leaned against it, allowing himself a moment to savor the silence. In just a few hours, the concourse would be filled with construction workers and shop owners. The noise would reach a deafening din and chaos would reign. He released a heavy sigh. There was still so much work to be done and less than two weeks in which to do it.

He headed for his office, sidestepping piles of lumber, equipment and packing crates before reaching the malfunctioning escalator in the center of the mall. The company had promised to replace its defective motor immediately. That had been two months ago, and every time he called, they said it was on its way. If every person he'd talked to at the company had been telling him the truth, he figured he'd receive about ten motors and, with any luck, one of them might work.

As he began to climb the steps, he recalled the series of bizarre catastrophes that had taken place in this project. It seemed as if his problems had begun the moment he'd marked the X on the calendar designating the day after Thanksgiving as the mall's official opening date.

The first disaster to befall him was that all fifty thousand sheets of stationery he'd ordered had arrived with his name printed as Adam Worse, which seemed morbidly apropos at the moment. Then the contractor had no more than poured the foundation when his workers had gone on a three-week strike to protest, of all things, a lack of portable toilets at the site. The strike should have been resolved within a few days, but for some unknown reason, there was a shortage of portable toilets all over the state. They finally managed to round up enough to satisfy the workers, only to be hit with a two-week rainy season the likes of which Colorado had never seen before. He should have expected a monsoon—after all, it never rains but it pours.

Finally the contractor and his people were able to go back to work. For the next several months, things had run smoothly if a sensible man—and Adam did consider himself a sensible man—made allowances for the normal glitches in construction. By the time his office was finished and he finally had a roof over his head, he was sure that his problems were under control.

He should have knocked on wood, he now thought grimly, because a month later his manager had been wooed away by the competition—or rather the competition's well-endowed daughter—and he hadn't been able to find a satisfactory replacement. And if that wasn't bad enough, this past Monday his Santa Claus had been arrested for drunk driving and was spending the next thirty days in jail. Now he not only had to find a replacement for him, but another portrait photographer to take the kids' pictures, since "Santa's" wife had had the job and she refused to work without her husband.

Adam shook his head in disgust. He was tempted to forgo the North Pole booth altogether, but one of the mall's biggest draws would be the kids having their picture taken with the jolly old man. Besides, he'd already sent out discount coupons for the photography sessions, and he knew from firsthand experience that hell hath no fury like shoppers who can't redeem their coupons.

It shouldn't be too difficult to find a new Santa, he reassured himself as he reached the second floor and rounded the corner leading to his office, but a portrait photographer was another matter. All the good ones had already been hired or were too busy with their own seasonal rush to take on a last-minute job. He'd find one eventually, even if he had to hire someone from out of town. It was frustrating to concede that if he had a manager, he wouldn't have to worry about the Santa problem—or a dozen others, for that matter.

He entered his office, took off his coat and grabbed the empty coffeepot. While he started the first brew of the day, he sent a prayer of thanks heavenward that his secretary wasn't averse to helping keep the pot full, because he survived on caffeine. He didn't even have time to make a trip to the nearest fast-food drive-in for lunch these days, which, he decided, was probably just as well. He'd most likely end up with food poisoning, though at the moment he found the prospect rather appealing. At least he'd be able to spend more than three or four hours in bed.

By the time he managed to drink half a pot of coffee and go through the remainder of yesterday's mail, his secretary, Vivian, arrived. They exchanged harried good-mornings. Before tackling his paperwork, Adam paused for a moment to wonder fatalistically what destiny had in store for him today. . . and shuddered at the thought.

"POP, WOULD YOU STOP complaining?" Christmas—Christy to her friends—Knight asked impatiently as she slammed her foot down on the gas pedal and shot through the third yellow light in a row. She disregarded her father's white-knuckled grip on the dashboard. "If you'd gotten your act together, we wouldn't be running behind. This appointment is critical to my career, and you know it."

Robert Knight glared at his daughter. "If I'd gotten my act together, I wouldn't even be in the car. I look ridiculous!"

Christy peered at him before shifting her Toyota coupe into second gear and careering around the corner. "You don't look ridiculous. You look like Santa Claus."

"I don't want to look like Santa Claus," he grumbled. "And your mother wouldn't let me put in a second pillow! When I stand up, my pants are going to fall down. I just know it!"

Christy couldn't control her grin. "*Then* you will look ridiculous. Unless, of course, you're wearing holiday boxer shorts," she teased. "You know, something with reindeer on it, or elves, or—"

"This isn't funny, Christy, and you shouldn't make fun of your father," he said with an indignant sniff.

"You're right, and I'm sorry." She reached over to squeeze his hand. "I really am. And I do appreciate you helping me out."

"Appreciate me more by watching where you're going!" he exclaimed as she swerved over the center line toward an oncoming car.

"Your wish is my command." She pulled back into her own lane while praying they'd make their interview on time.

The moment Christy had heard about Evergreen Mall's loss of their Santa team, she'd been determined to land the job. It was the perfect opportunity to promote her newly opened portrait studio. Still, it had taken her all week to persuade her father, who was normally putty in her hands, to agree to don a Santa suit. In the last few years he'd let both his white hair and beard grow unfashionably long, and his seasoned paunch had required little padding. His reference to needing a second pillow had made Christy realize that that was why he'd refused to help in the first place. His portly ego was being placed on the line, and he didn't like to think he could fill the jolly man's pants. But Christy knew that the moment the first little girl or boy climbed onto his knee, her father would be in seventh heaven. She reached over and gave his hand another squeeze.

"The secretary said the west entrance would be the only one open," she told him as the mall came into sight. "I wonder which one that is?"

"West is always toward the mountains, remember?" her father said with a resigned sigh.

"How could I have forgotten? I guess three years back east messed up my directional signals."

"That's not all it messed up," Robert groused when she took another corner with the daring expertise of a New York City cabdriver. "You drive like a bat out of hell. If you don't slow down, we'll never make it to your interview."

Christy didn't bother to respond—her father's grumbling was just a quirk of his personality. Beneath his gruff exterior was a heart so full of love it had to be twice the normal size.

She fondly looked over at him. All her life she'd been closer to her parents than most children. Ilona and Robert Knight had been married for twenty-four years before she'd come along. The doctors had called her a late-in-life baby, but her parents had called her a miracle. When she was born on Christmas Day, they'd named her after the holiday and spent the next twenty-two years showering her with their love.

But when she'd graduated from college three years ago with a degree in photographic journalism, she'd realized it was time to cut the apron strings and had accepted a training position in Philadelphia with a firm of free-lance photographers. The job had not only offered her a chance to obtain a wide variety of photographic experience, but more important, it had allowed her to do some growing up.

From the beginning she had recognized that free-lance photography wouldn't be her lifelong career. Then, when her father had suffered a heart attack six months ago, she'd resigned and moved back to Colorado Springs. She was determined to give her elderly parents the nurturing and support they had so unselfishly given her over the years. Which was another reason why she needed this job. The doctor felt that the part-time work would be good therapy for her seventy-year-old father, who'd been prone to periods of depression since his heart attack. Christy was convinced that playing Santa Claus would put new spring in his step and bring back the vitality that had been missing since his illness. Quite simply, he needed something to take his mind off his health and make him feel useful again.

"Are you ready?" she asked as she pulled into a parking space. Her father's answer was an unintelligible growl, and she leaned over to plant a kiss on his cheek. "Thanks for doing this, Pop. It means a lot to me."

"Let's just get it over with," he responded, opening his door and heaving himself out of the car. "This Santa suit is costing us by the hour."

Christy climbed out of the car and joined him, shivering as the cold wind whipped around her green tights-clad legs.

"Where's your coat?" Robert asked with parental disapproval as he scrutinized her brief elf costume.

"A coat would ruin the effect," she answered, tucking her portfolio beneath her arm and hurrying toward the mall.

"And pneumonia could kill you." He draped his arm around her shoulders, pulling her close to protect her from the wind. "You can't work if you're flat on your back in bed."

She gave his pillowed stomach a teasing push with her finger. "Don't worry about me. I'm as healthy as a horse."

"I'll believe that when you have four legs and a permanent fur coat." He opened the mall door and shoved her through it.

Christy halted inside the entrance, shaking her head as her ears were assaulted by the noise of pounding hammers and buzzing saws and sneezing as sawdust tickled her nose. But she grinned when three construction workers stopped to stare and whistle at her.

Robert immediately grabbed her arm and pulled her toward the center of the mall. The secretary had said the main office was up the escalator and to the right, and he couldn't seem to move in that direction fast enough.

"Hey, slow down!" she exclaimed, trotting to keep up with his long-legged stride.

"You should have worn a coat," he muttered, scowling in the direction of another set of workers who were eyeing Christy. There was another wolf whistle, and she impishly glanced over her shoulder and waved at the men. "Christmas!" her father chastised in parental horror.

"Oh, come on, Pop. They're only having some fun."

"Your mother would have a heart attack if she saw you behaving like this."

Christy didn't bother to correct him. She'd inherited her legs from her mother, who still received her share of appreciative stares at the age of sixty-eight. She also knew that her mother enjoyed every one of them, but it was the best-kept secret in the house. Her father was as jealous of his wife as he'd been fifty years ago, and her mother adored him for it.

Christy led the way up the dead escalator to the second floor. They followed the arrowed signs to the mall's office. Before opening the door, she adjusted her elf cap. The secretary looked up absently at first, then smiled in amusement.

"You must be Ms. Knight," she said.

"Yes, and this is my father, Santa Claus," Christy replied with a laugh.

Robert gave a disgruntled "Harrumph."

The secretary's smile widened. "Mr. Worth's on the phone. Why don't you have a seat? It's been so hectic today, I forgot to tell him about your appointment. It may take a few minutes."

"I've got all day," Christy said, sitting on the low sofa in the corner and patting the cushion beside her. She ignored her father's mutterings about how he'd been exposed to her hair-raising driving skills and brushes with death just to have to sit and wait.

The woman rose from her chair and entered a door behind her desk. Several minutes passed, and Christy tried to calm her nerves. It had been a long time since she'd had a job interview, and she found it a bit intimidating. No matter how hard she tried, she couldn't ease her grip on the portfolio lying on her lap.

Smile, she told herself, and her lips automatically obeyed the command. Her motto had always been: When In Doubt, Put Up A Good Front. It hadn't failed her yet.

Finally, there was a low murmur and then a masculine voice became audible. "I won't hire any more teams. I want a separate Santa and a separate photographer. That way, if one doesn't work out, I'm not beating the bushes for both. Thank these people for coming, but tell them I'm not interested."

Christy looked at her father in disappointment. She'd been confident that once Mr. Worth saw her work he'd hire her, and that he'd never be able to come up with a more realistic-looking Santa than her father. Her father stared back at her, his own disappointment evident in his eyes. She realized that despite his grumbling, he'd been looking forward to the job. And, darn it, he needed it for his emotional health! she thought in frustration.

Suddenly her father's lips tightened into a determined line, and he pushed himself to the edge of the sofa and then to his feet, teetering precariously for a moment. Christy reached out to steady him. As soon as his feet were firmly planted, he grabbed her arm and pulled her up beside him. With a jolly "Ho! Ho! Ho!" he barged into the back office, dragging Christy along with him.

When Christy figured out what her father was up to, she was momentarily appalled. Then she decided, what the heck. They couldn't get the job without meeting Mr. Worth, and if she played her cards right, she might be able to change the man's mind about hiring a team.

ADAM GLANCED UP from his secretary, ready to give the intruders his strongest look of censure. Before he could, a huge Santa Claus reached across the desk, grasped his hand and pumped it furiously.

"Robert Knight at your service, Mr. Worth." He dropped Adam's hand and pushed an elf toward his desk. "This is my daughter. The best portrait photographer in town."

Adam parted his lips to ask them to leave, but the young woman grabbed his hand and shook it with the same enthusiasm as her father.

"You don't know how nice it is to meet you, Mr. Worth. I can tell by looking at you that we're going to enjoy doing business together," she told him.

"But—" Adam began, only to be cut off by Robert Knight.

"Christy, show Mr. Worth your photographs."

"Of course."

Adam's gaze was drawn to her rounded posterior as she placed a portfolio on the chair behind her and bent over to unzip it. *Nice legs, too*, he decided, giving them an equally appreciative appraisal. When she turned to face him, he let his gaze slowly rise, taking in the rest of her. *Small and compact, but devastating all the same.* He experienced a flash of desire, and shifted self-consciously in his chair before he looked at her face. If a stranger could have this much effect on him, he'd better do something about his social life.

"I, uh, suppose it wouldn't hurt to look at your work," he admitted.

"It's painless," she replied, as her smile curved into a grin and she rounded his desk to drop a photograph in front of him.

He forced himself to focus on the child's picture, which was quite a feat after her perfume hit him. Some type of musk, he'd guess, and it was doing crazy things to his libido. He most definitely needed to improve his social life. "It's very good."

"Actually, it's the worst of the lot," she commented while adjusting the cap over her upswept blond hair. "There are eleven better ones." She began dropping them down on his desk.

Each was a better photo than the last. Adam was amazed that she seemed to have captured the unique personality of every child in turn. He'd always been fond of children, and he smiled as he dug back through the pictures, picking out a puckish dark-haired girl with a mischievous grin. The child reminded Adam of his half sister, Danielle, when she'd been that age, and he picked up the photograph and leaned back in his chair to study it.

Christy sat on the edge of his desk and swung her legs while he contemplated the picture. Mr. Adam Worth was much younger than she'd expected—about twenty years younger. She gauged him to be somewhere in his late thirties, and she would have loved to spend an hour with him in front of the camera. He had medium brown hair highlighted with glints of gold. His features were well-defined—a square chin and jaw, a straight nose—and his eyes were a melting cocoa-brown. From what she could see of his upper torso beneath his navy blue sport coat, the camera wouldn't balk at the rest of him, either.

Suddenly he looked up at her and his smile widened. If the cleft in his chin was breathtaking, his dimple was absolutely devastating.

"You're an excellent photographer, Ms. . . ."

"Knight with a *K*. Christmas Knight," she added, realizing they hadn't been properly introduced. "And thanks for the compliment."

He nodded as his gaze was drawn to her swinging legs. They were the best legs he'd ever seen, and he had to fight the urge to reach out and touch them. He cleared his throat and looked back at her. "Your name is unusual."

She laughed. "You can blame that on Pop. He's the one who chose it."

He observed her father. The man did make a nice Santa Claus with his flowing white hair and busy beard. Too bad he'd resolved not to hire another team.

"I'm sorry," he announced, "but even though you appear to be qualified for the job, I'm not in the market for a team."

It was time to take the offensive, and even though Christy knew the answer, she asked, "Why?"

Adam's smile was grim. "I've had bad luck with teams."

"If you're talking about the Hendersons, let me assure you that my father is quite sober. He has two or three social drinks a year, and the rest of the time he lives on cranberry juice."

"It's good for the kidneys," Robert inserted quickly, justifying his fondness for the juice.

Adam chuckled. "So I've heard, but I'm still not—."

"You can't make up your mind until you've heard our terms," Christy interrupted, her mind racing as she tried to come up with some. She *had* to have this job. Without it, she'd have to dip into her savings to pay her bills, and she didn't want to do that. She wanted to keep it as an emergency fund to tide her over during the lean months that bedeviled every portrait photographer's life. And, she reminded herself again, her father needed the work for his emotional well-being. That made her even more determined to change Adam Worth's mind.

"I assure you it won't make any difference," Adam said.

"But you'll listen to them, anyway, right?"

He cast a reluctant glance at his watch. "I can spare five minutes."

"I've seen your discount coupons. Am I right to assume that you were going to reimburse the Hendersons out of your own pocket?" He nodded, and she continued, "Well, we'll honor the discount coupons and absorb the cost ourselves."

"You can afford to do that?"

"I can't afford not to. I need this job. We'll also foot the candy bill for the kids out of our percentage of the take."

"And what kind of percentage are we talking about?" he asked cautiously, certain that this was the kicker.

She began to swing her legs again, smiling when his gaze drifted toward them. She knew it was a dirty trick, but she was desperate, and desperate situations demanded drastic measures. She crossed her legs and ran her hand from her ankle to her knee as if smoothing out wrinkles. She got the reaction she wanted: His pupils dilated. "The same as you were going to give the Hendersons."

"I still don't know," he replied, his gaze glued to her legs, but Christy could tell he was wavering.

With him teetering on the brink, she had to give him a push. "I'll make you a deal you can't refuse," she told him, grinning.

He laughed then, and she marveled at the hearty sound. There was a decided lack of laugh lines at the corners of his mouth and his eyes, which meant he laughed rarely. She wondered why. If she got the job, she might have occasion to find out. She slid off his desk, placed her palms on it and leaned toward him to gain his complete attention.

Adam found himself staring into sapphire-blue eyes so pure in color that they rivaled the gem. Suddenly he realized how beautiful she was, with her small heart-shaped face, sinfully long lashes, and Cupid's-bow lips. An image of her upswept hair loose and tangled around her shoulders flashed through his mind, and he gulped. Her legs were great, but her face was fantastic. Why hadn't he noticed that earlier?

"Uh, what deal?" he asked, leaning back in his chair as he tried unsuccessfully to break the mesmerizing hold her eyes had on him.

"I'll give you insurance."

"Insurance?"

She nodded. "You estimate how much you think your take will be, and I'll match it with my own money. Then, if we don't live up to our contract, you get to keep it."

Adam arched his brows. He wasn't about to take her "insurance" money, and he couldn't help being suspicious of the offer. Granted, taking pictures of kids with Santa could be quite lucrative, but it wasn't lucrative enough to risk losing your own dough. However, her offer did make him understand how badly she wanted the job.

"I don't know," he said again, even though—despite his better judgment—he was going to hire the Knights. He needed a good photographer, and if her portraits were a true indication of her talent, she was better than good. He'd be a fool to let her get away.

Christy looked down at her watch. "We still have two minutes. You can use those to make up your mind. Pop and I don't mind waiting."

Her smile made Adam burst into laughter. If nothing else, she was persistent, and he admired persistence. "I'll have my secretary draw up a contract and mail it to you."

"Great!" Christy exclaimed, refraining from clapping her hands in victory. "When do you want my insurance money?"

"Keep it in the bank. I'll trust you to pay me if the time comes."

Christy sobered. Considering his recent debacle with the Hendersons, she was surprised that he was being so generous. In his place, she wasn't sure she would have been, particularly when dealing with an unknown entity.

"You won't regret hiring us, Mr. Worth," she told him sincerely.

Adam didn't know why, but he believed her. He smiled ruefully when he realized that he hadn't asked her for references. For all he knew, she hadn't even taken the portraits she was stuffing back into her portfolio.

"I'm sure I won't," he said. He didn't need references. After all, beggars couldn't be choosers, and right now he was begging for a photographer. "I'll expect you here bright and early on the Friday after Thanksgiving. In the meantime, we'll be in touch on the details of the North Pole booth. If you need anything special, let me know."

"All I need is a chair for Santa," she commented as she zipped her portfolio closed and tucked it beneath her arm.

Adam rose to his feet and accepted Robert Knight's hand. Then he took Christy's, holding it longer than necessary, but she didn't seem to object. As he gazed into her eyes, he felt a strange kind of connection—as if he'd known her before. It was ridiculous, of course. He would have remembered this woman who exuded so much femininity that it warmed his blood.

"Nice doing business with you, Mr. Worth," Christy said, slipping her hand from his. She'd not only enjoyed his touch, but had found it disconcerting. His hand was large and warm, and she'd experienced a strange tingling sensation as he'd clasped hers. She'd never had anything like that happen before, and she rubbed her palm against her thigh as she regarded him.

"The same here," Adam replied. "And please call me Adam."

When she smiled, she looked years older than she had the moment before. Adam was curious as to just how old she was.

"Twenty-five," she said, startling him.

"Excuse me?"

Her seemingly ever-present grin was in place. "I recognized the look. I'm twenty-five years old, and my mother assures me that as the years pass, I'll be happy about looking younger than my age."

Adam returned her grin. "I'm sure you will, Ms. Knight."

"Christy," she corrected. "See you the Friday after Thanksgiving."

"Bright and early," he reminded, unable to keep his eyes off her shapely legs as she took her father's arm and walked out of his office.

Adam dropped back into his chair, grinning when he heard her muffled "Wahoo!" filter in from the corridor. He'd just performed one of the craziest, most unprofessional acts of his life by hiring the Knights on sheer impulse. He prayed he wasn't going to regret it.

2

ADAM WAS STILL CURSING the fact that he hadn't found a manager as he supervised the mounting of the elaborate Christmas decorations he'd purchased. There was so much paperwork waiting for him upstairs that he was surprised his desk wasn't sagging beneath the weight. He'd spent a fortune on the mall's decorations, however, and wasn't about to let the work crew deck the halls alone.

By the time the day was over, he expected Evergreen Mall to be living up to its name. Each of the four entrances would be flanked by two giant potted evergreens decorated from top to bottom, but none of them would compare to the mammoth Christmas tree that would stand in the center of the mall.

The mall's second level had a child-size train that would travel from one end to the other through a world of moving, talking toys. Each concourse on the main level was being decorated with a theme in mind. One would represent the religious holiday of Christ's birth. Another would represent Hanukkah—the Jewish festival of lights. Still another was devoted to a winter wonderland, complete with mechanical mannequins building snowmen, sleigh riding and ice-skating.

The most elaborate decorations, however, were located at the "North Pole," where mechanical elves were hard at work in Santa's workshop and loading his sleigh. Reindeer—real reindeer—grazed outside, waiting to give rides to visiting children. Santa Claus would be sitting in a homey living room beside a floor-to-ceiling picture window that looked out on a snow-covered background.

Adam knew he'd gone overboard with the decorations, but he'd justified the expense by telling himself that they'd last for years. He also wanted to make Evergreen Mall a showplace—a must-see for everyone. It was an odd goal that he hadn't quite resolved within himself since he knew his "Bah, humbug!" attitude rivaled Scrooge's. Yet there was also a secret part of him that always whispered, *This year the holidays will be different. This time they'll be fun and happy.* But they never were different. They were always miserable. So why was he going through with this ridiculous charade?

He was simply using sound marketing techniques, he reassured himself as he argued with the work crew decorating the central Christmas tree. After he won the argument, he glanced at his watch. Christy Knight would be arriving at any moment.

He headed for the west entrance to keep her from making the unnecessary journey to his office. Why had he summoned her in the first place? He could have handled their business by telephone, but for some crazy reason, he'd wanted to discuss his plans with her in person.

Six days had passed since he'd hired her. He dismissed the strange exhilaration he felt at seeing her again, telling himself it was simply a reaction to the adrenaline rush of supervising all the work at hand. But that didn't slow his half-running gait, nor did it prevent a smile of anticipation from springing to his lips.

ONCE AGAIN CHRISTY ARRIVED at Evergreen Mall. This time, she was dressed in comfortable denims tucked into knee-high winter boots, and a fisherman's-knit sweater worn over a peach cashmere turtleneck. Her hair was tucked beneath a matching peach knit cap.

There was no wind, and the sun was blinding against the snow that had fallen the week before. She pushed her sunglasses up the bridge of her nose as she surveyed the huge mound of plowed snow that stretched the length of the parking lot and ended at the main entrance to the mall. A dozen men stood on top of it and were packing it down with the enthusiasm of a highway construction crew building a road.

She paused in her walk across the parking lot and stuffed her hands into her back pockets as she watched them work. What in the world were they up to? It would take forever for that mound to melt, and it blocked the access road that ran in front of the mall. Shoppers would not only have to drive around it, but it took up at least two, maybe three, prime parking lanes.

With a confused shake of her head, she continued toward the mall, pondering why Adam Worth had summoned her. She'd signed the contract and mailed it back three days ago. Then, yesterday, she'd returned from taking pictures at a wedding to find an urgent message from him on her answering machine. When she'd called him back, his secretary had informed her that he was out of the office but that he wanted to see her at nine the next morning.

She glanced at her watch and cursed when she discovered it was two minutes to nine. Instinct told her that punctuality was a must with her new boss, and she broke into a dead run, not slowing down until she flung open the mall door and promptly collided with a large, masculine body.

A pair of strong arms encircled her, and she braced her hands against a wide chest. As she fought to catch her breath, she found herself staring at a red-and-blue-checked flannel shirt that clung to an impressive set of pectoral muscles. As she lifted her gaze, catching a glimpse of golden brown chest hair at the open neck of the shirt, an ominous feeling of recognition rushed through her. Sure enough, it was Adam Worth. To her relief, he was smiling.

"I'd ask if the building was on fire, but it couldn't be since you're coming in instead of going out," he said, unwrapping one arm.

"I'm running late," Christy explained, knowing she should be pulling away from his embrace, but finding it rather pleasant to be in his arms. "I would have been on time, but I stopped to watch those men working on your snow mountain in the parking lot. What are they doing?"

"Building a road for Santa's sleigh," Adam answered. He was enjoying the sensation of her soft body leaning against him, and he reluctantly released his hold on her when a crew of workmen exited a nearby shop and eyed them curiously.

As he stepped away from her, he looked at her face. She was as beautiful as he remembered, and he found himself wishing that he'd removed her sunglasses so he could see her eyes. He also wanted to jerk off her cap to see exactly how long her hair was. Was it shoulder length, as he'd guessed, or longer? Without even realizing what he was doing, he reached out to caress a silken strand that had escaped from her cap before tucking it back into place.

"Santa's sleigh?" Christy echoed, feeling oddly breathless as his warm fingers skimmed along the crest of her ear and the side of her neck. It was only a reaction to her running, she rationalized. She wasn't used to such vigorous activity. Then she admitted she was lying to herself.

"Yes, Santa's sleigh. That's why I wanted to see you." He stuffed his hands into the pockets of his jeans and tried to ignore the impact the woman was having on him. "I thought I might as well take advantage of all this snow. On opening day, I want you and your father to arrive at the front door in a sleigh pulled by four reindeer."

"Real reindeer?" she asked, finding herself just as captivated by his handsome face as she'd been the day she'd met him about the job. Once again, she longed to get him in front of a camera, and she lowered her eyes to study the rest of him. His body—in the tailored flannel shirt, stone-washed denims and scuffed cowboy boots—was model perfect, and she sighed remembering the feel of hard masculine muscle pressed against her. The man was not only photogenic, but beefcake material, too.

"Real reindeer. I know this isn't in our contract, and if you want to renegotiate—"

"Where did you find real reindeer?" she interrupted.

"At the unemployment office. Where else?" he returned without cracking a smile, but the laughter in his eyes told her he'd just made a joke.

Christy grinned, pleased by his show of humor. "Of course. How silly of me. Everyone knows that's the first place you look for reindeer. Do they bite?"

He shrugged. "I don't know. I didn't ask."

"In that case, we'll have to negotiate for medical benefits."

"Medical benefits?" he repeated warily.

"Everyone knows that a reindeer bite can be very dangerous," she explained, injecting just the right amount of concern into her voice. She knew she shouldn't be teasing him, but she wanted to hear him laugh. "You see, only recently scientists have discovered that there are several dangerous and heretofore unknown viruses that thrive in reindeer. I'm afraid the cure for their bite is expensive, because the ingredients are rare. You need two tablespoons of ground mistletoe, a teaspoon of—"

"Ground mistletoe?" he interjected with a delighted laugh, fulfilling Christy's wish. "I'm not that gullible, so you can stop pulling my leg."

She glanced down at his legs and then slid her gaze slowly upward. Adam's pulse quickened, and there was a tightening in his loins that he prayed wasn't visible. He cursed the fact that her eyes were still shielded behind her sunglasses. Was she teasing him, or flirting with him?

"Pulling your leg might be an interesting proposition," she drawled.

"You're too young for interesting propositions," he stated gruffly.

"Is that right? How old would I have to be to get an interesting proposition from you?"

Good heavens, she *was* flirting with him! And his libido became even more insistent. He'd better put a stop to this conversation right here and now. He had only one hard-and-fast rule in life, and that was that he *never* dated a woman more than five years younger than him. He'd watched his father struggle through a second marriage with a woman ten years his junior, and he'd witnessed the seemingly insurmountable problems they'd faced because of their age difference. "A lot older. I'm thirty-seven."

"Wow!" Christy exclaimed, grinning. "Have you signed up for your senior-citizen discounts yet?"

Adam scowled at her. "I'm not saying that I'm old. I'm saying that I'm too old for *you*."

"I see." She pursed her lips. "So if I was five years older, you'd be amenable to offering me an interesting proposition?"

"More like seven years," Adam revised.

"Aha. A five-year age difference is your limit." She stepped close to him, and Adam gulped as her musky perfume teased at his nose. "I don't suppose you believe in that old saying that you're only as old as you feel."

All Adam could do was shake his head, because at that moment he felt like a teenager in his sexual prime. He stuffed his hands into his back pockets, because he wanted to jerk her into his arms and kiss her until she couldn't breathe. What was happening to him? He never lost control of his libido. Never! But Lord, she was gorgeous. He'd have to be dead not to respond to her.

"What if I told you that I adore older men?" she suggested in a sultry voice that made the hair on the back of his neck stand on end. What it did to the rest of his body was downright scandalous, and he took a cautious step back from her.

"I'd say, 'What would your father say?'"

She chuckled. "He'd probably say exactly what he says about all the men in my life."

"Which is?"

"'What in the world do you see in him?'"

Adam couldn't help smiling as an image of Robert Knight flashed through his mind. He could see the man saying exactly that, though he had a feeling that in this instance, the man's words might be a bit stronger. "He's overprotective, huh?"

"Afraid so."

"I don't blame him. If I had a little girl like you, I'd be overprotective, too."

Christy pulled off her sunglasses and gazed up at him seriously. "Then you'd be making the same mistake he is. I am not a little girl, Adam. I'm a full-grown woman quite capable of making my own decisions in life."

Adam gulped again as he stared down into her bright blue eyes, because the maturity in their depths more than convinced him that what she'd said was true. She was most assuredly a full-grown woman, and he was responding to her as a full-grown man. He also knew that if he even tried to act upon the provocative impulses he was experiencing, her father would probably shoot him.

The sensual spell she'd woven around him was broken when she said, "Now, tell me about this grand entrance you want me and my father to make."

Adam had to draw in a deep breath and let it out slowly before he could speak. "I thought it would be nice if Santa made a newsworthy arrival at Evergreen Mall." He began to stroll toward the center of the mall, needing to work off the tension that had sprung up between them.

Christy walked beside him, only half listening to his plans. The other half was centered on Adam as she tried to figure out why she felt so drawn to him. The absence of laugh lines in his face indicated that he was much too serious for her. She also knew today's attire was an anomaly; most of the time he'd be wearing stuffy three-piece suits and wing-tip shoes. She liked men who laughed easily and led casual lives.

But she was very aware of the strong masculinity Adam exuded, and she was intrigued by the glimpses she'd seen of his humor, which indicated the potential for laughter was there. This made him a mystery, and Christy loved mysteries. She couldn't wait to begin tugging at the threads that would unravel the one surrounding Adam. She also couldn't wait to find out if he was as good a kisser as she imagined he would be.

"SCROOGE AT FOUR o'clock!" Robert Knight called out, and Christy looked up from the child she was talking to, searching for Adam, whom her father had dubbed Scrooge.

She smiled when she saw him standing head and shoulders above the crowd. Two days ago, Santa and elf had arrived by sled to the cheers of hundreds of children, and Christy and her father had been working hard ever since. Already her father's spirits had improved a hundred percent, and Christy, too, was enjoying the job. But it was Adam's frequent visits to the booth that she enjoyed the most. Her father, however, insisted that Adam was spying on them.

Christy sensed that his visits were much more personal in nature. Though she'd have liked to believe that it was because Adam wanted to see her, she'd concluded that it was the children drawing him. His expression always softened when he looked at them, and several times she'd seen him reach out as if to brush a child's hair into place only to restrain himself before he could complete the gesture.

The little girl beside her was becoming restless, and Christy reminded herself that she was here to take pictures, not to ogle Adam—even if it was a pleasurable pastime. She led the child to her father just as Adam arrived.

Adam rested against the railing surrounding the North Pole booth and smiled as he watched Christy and Robert tease a sober-looking little girl into smiles and laughter. Several more children followed before there was a lull, and Christy changed the film in her camera before approaching him.

"What's up, boss?" she asked with a cheeky grin.

He shrugged and attempted to suppress the flare of desire he experienced whenever he was around her. "The usual. How's business?"

"Booming. Pop's knee is about to give out." Christy knew she'd just made a faux pas when Adam immediately looked at her father with concern. She touched his arm. "That was a joke, Adam."

"You're sure?" he asked. His gaze was drawn back to her hand where she touched him. It was such a small hand, and he wanted to run his fingers across it, to trace its delicate veins.

She's off-limits, Adam told himself for at least the millionth time in the past two days, but he sensed he was fighting a losing battle. The more he was around Christy, the more enchanted he became with her. And it wasn't just physical; she had the knack of making him laugh, and laughter had always been a rare commodity in his life. But even more appealing was her serenity; nothing seemed to rattle her. It was a personality trait Adam would have given his eyeteeth for in his overstressed life.

"Positive," she assured in answer to his question. Then she teasingly asked, "Want your picture taken with Santa?"

He frowned. "Of course not."

"Why not? Surely you want to ask Santa for a special gift for Christmas. You know—something tall, dark and slinky."

He returned his attention to her and grinned. "That wouldn't be a bad request, but we both know there isn't a Santa Claus."

"Who told you that?" she demanded, widening her eyes to ridiculous proportions, while wondering if "tall, dark and slinky" was the type of woman he liked. Heavens, she hoped not, because as crazy as it seemed, she was becoming infatuated with the man. The problem was, he was so darned busy that she never got a chance to spend more than a few minutes with him. But she was going to find a way to spend some time with him, she promised herself. How else was she going to find out if he was a good kisser?

"My father," he replied in answer to her question.

"And he's a practical man just like you, right?"

She was surprised to see a series of emotions flicker through his eyes, but they were gone before she could interpret them. He looked away from her, and she had a feeling that it wasn't the crowd he saw.

"No," he corrected softly, almost sadly. "My father is a realist." Before Christy could respond, he glanced down at his watch and said, "Damn, I'm late for an appointment. Call Vivian if you have any problems."

He rushed down the corridor, leaving her gazing after him thoughtfully.

"What's the matter with him?" Robert asked as he joined her.

"I don't think he knows how to dream," she answered. Not wanting to elaborate on her statement since she wasn't sure what she meant, she added, "You'd better get back to your chair. Here comes a mama bear with six baby bears, and she looks frenzied."

"If I had six kids, I wouldn't be frenzied. I'd be suicidal," Robert commented as he returned to his post.

An hour and a half later, Robert went home for lunch, and Christy wandered down to Bertha's Mexican Hat to eat. She sat on a stool at the counter and watched Bertha

Gonzales expertly prepare six burritos for another customer. When the customer was gone, Bertha approached Christy with a weary smile.

"Business is booming, and my feet are killing me," she complained.

"Where's Suzanne?" Christy asked, referring to the woman's daughter who normally helped at the small take-out restaurant.

"Getting some Christmas shopping done. Do you want the usual?"

"Yes, thanks."

She was silent while Bertha put together a medium-size tostada and added an extra dollop of the guacamole Christy so dearly loved. After serving Christy, Bertha waited on a few more customers before returning to talk to her.

"I'm hearing good reports on Santa Claus."

Christy smiled. "I knew Pop was perfect for the role. So far, we've only had one sobbing toddler, but he managed to calm her down. He grumbles a lot, but he has a magic touch when it comes to kids."

Bertha nodded. "Adam Worth said the same thing."

"He did?" Christy questioned in surprise. "When?"

"A couple of hours ago when he stopped by to see how I was doing. Suzanne's going to have a fit when she finds out he was here and she missed him. She has a bad case of puppy love for him."

"He's a little old for her, isn't he?" Christy ventured, picturing the pretty, black-haired eighteen-year-old. Suzanne would definitely fall into the category "tall, dark and slinky," and Christy frowned at the twinge of annoyance that thought brought on. She also reminded herself that she sounded just like Adam. Age didn't have a blessed thing to do with a relationship between a man and a woman, and despite Adam's claims to the contrary, she had a feeling he'd change his tune if the right woman came along. The twinge of annoyance grew.

Bertha chuckled. "You and I know that he's too old for her, but try telling Suzanne. She spends all her free time upstairs with his secretary under the guise of trying to develop her secretarial skills. She thinks I'm too old and foolish to understand that she's really up there pumping Vivian for every bit of information she can get on Adam."

"And what has she learned?" Christy inquired.

"He's gotten to you, too?" Bertha asked in amazement.

"Of course not," Christy lied. "I'm just like any other red-blooded employee. I like to hear all the juicy gossip about the boss."

Bertha's knowing grin was wide as she braced both elbows on the counter and moved closer, lowering her voice to a conspiratorial level. "Well, according to Suzanne, who of course learned everything from Vivian, Adam has never been married and desperately needs a woman to look after him."

"Desperately?" Christy repeated with a dubious shake of her head. "I doubt that. He looks capable of handling almost anything, and I'm sure he has plenty of women waiting in the wings to do whatever he doesn't want to do."

"I think you're wrong there. According to Vivian, the mall is his life. She says he rarely dates, and I tend to believe that."

"Oh, come on, Bertha," Christy objected. "You've seen the man. He's heartbreaker gorgeous!"

"Yes," Bertha agreed. "But he practically lives here. My husband and I had to come in at four one morning to meet some deliverymen, and the security guard told us that Adam had arrived just a few minutes before us. You also know that I stay open until after the movie-theater crowd goes home. Then I have to clean up and get everything ready for the next day. Sometimes it's after midnight before I get out of here, and when I drive out of the parking lot, I'll invariably see the light on in Adam's office."

"No wonder he's always so serious," Christy murmured as she mulled over the information. "All work and no play would make any man a Scrooge."

"You'd better believe it," Bertha said. "Want a refill on that iced tea?"

"No," Christy answered. "Pop will be back any minute, and he refuses to set foot inside the booth until I'm there. He's afraid of the reindeer stabled next to us."

"Afraid of the reindeer?" Bertha echoed in astonishment. "But the kids ride them! They're so gentle, they almost purr!"

"I know. But Pop has this theory that reindeer are related to bulls. Therefore, he's certain that red will set them off and they'll charge him. He says he's too old and out of shape to be a matador, so he's had me practicing with a throw rug out in the garage. I'm becoming quite the expert matadoress. Not one old, beat-up spare tire has gotten the best of me yet."

Bertha burst into laughter. "You and your father are crazy!"

Christy chuckled. "I know. It runs in the family."

"What runs in the family?" a familiar, husky baritone demanded.

Christy glanced up in surprise and found herself staring right into Adam's beautiful brown eyes. Her pulse began to race and her mind went blank, but he continued to regard her, waiting for her answer. She forced her brain back into operation. Controlling her heartbeat wasn't as easy.

"Insanity," she replied with an impish grin. "Looking for Suzanne?"

He placed an elbow on the counter and said in confusion, "Suzanne?"

"Suzanne," she repeated, pleased that he appeared to be genuinely at a loss. "You know—Bertha's tall, dark and slinky daughter who is so impressed with your business acumen that you've brought out the hidden secretarial aspirations in her."

"Did you really say all that in one breath?" he asked, returning her grin.

She loved it when he smiled. It did such marvelous things to his face. Wanting to see it stay in place, she announced, "I have a black belt in long-breath sentences. It took me years to earn it, but I can talk two bricks into crumbling pieces in ten seconds flat."

Adam chuckled and shook his head. Her quick humor was refreshing, and he wondered if she ever had a bad day. He had a feeling that one of her bad days would be equivalent to one of his good ones, and he had to fight the urge to trace the smiling curve of her lips with his fingertips.

"What does insanity running in the family have to do with Suzanne?" he questioned.

"It's a private joke. Walk me back to my camera?"

"Sure." He assisted her off the stool and fell into step beside her after they'd told Bertha goodbye.

Christy was quiet for several moments, just enjoying walking next to him and imagining what it would be like if he draped his arm around her shoulders. Some day she'd find out, but for now she'd better start some conversation. The more she knew about him, the better off she'd be, and the first thing she was going to do was confirm the workaholic tendencies Bertha had told her about.

"What do you do for fun, Adam?" she asked.

"Fun?" he echoed, as if the word was foreign.

"Fun. You know, those activities that you indulge yourself in, which have no redeeming value, but provide lighthearted amusement."

His smile returned. "You sound like a dictionary."

"I visit the bookstore a lot. Having an elf browsing through the shelves is excellent for business. So?"

"So what?" he murmured, finding himself mesmerized. She was so full of life and laughter that he tended to look at her as a whole rather than by her separate physical attributes. Then he'd unexpectedly find himself concentrating on her face, and he was always stunned by her beauty. What would she do if he pulled her into his arms to find out if her lips were as soft as they looked?

He blinked away the fantasy when Christy prompted, "Fun, remember?"

"Ah, yes. Fun." He tossed back the tails of his suit coat and stuffed his hands into his pants pockets, not sure how to answer her question. For most of his life he'd done nothing but work—scrimping and saving and investing his money so he could open his own mall.

"I guess I do what most people do," he finally said.

"Really? I would never have taken you for the orgy type."

Christy had to bite back her grin at his stunned expression. Even though she chastised herself for teasing him, she couldn't ignore the irresistible impulse to do so. With any luck, she'd get another laugh out of him.

"But then, as my mother always says, you can never recognize 'most people' by looks alone," she told him blithely. "That's why a girl has to be so careful these days."

Adam parted his lips to speak, but she rushed on with, "Of course, you don't look like a bowler, either, but I bet your average is 170, right?" He once again tried to speak, but she didn't even pause for breath. "And golf? No, you wouldn't play golf. Boxing would be more your style. I think . . ."

The only way he was going to get a word in edgewise was to shut her up, so he took her arm and placed his fingers against her lips.

Christy stared up at him, her heart leaping and her stomach quivering. His touch rattled her senses, but it was the look in his eyes that made her head reel. They were filled with amusement and something much deeper, much darker. Desire. It was the first time Adam had revealed the fact that he shared the attraction, and it pleased her so much, she wanted to throw her arms around his neck and kiss him until he couldn't breathe.

It also made her more determined than ever to pursue him—even if it meant kidnapping from his office at midnight. Heavens, that sounded like fun!

As Adam gazed down at her upturned face, he was assaulted with a need to kiss her that was so great it caused a tremor to race through him. He wanted to remove her ridiculous hat, pull the pins out of her hair and let his fingers glide through it. He wanted to feel her lips warm and pliant beneath his. He wanted—

He was jerked back to reality when his name came out over the paging system. He dropped his hand from Christy's mouth and quickly stepped away from her, barely able to restrain himself from raking his hand through his hair. She was more dangerous than he'd realized, because she'd made him forget that they were standing in the middle of a busy mall—and he didn't believe in public displays of affection.

Affection? he questioned ruefully. Hell, he'd been tempted to ravish her right where she stood. Fortunately Vivian had come to the rescue by paging him, because if she hadn't, he would probably have ended up making a spectacle of himself. From now on, he vowed, he was going to keep his distance from Christy, because if he didn't, he had a feeling he'd be stepping into quicksand.

Christy wanted to wail in frustration. He'd come so close to kissing her, and then that damnable paging system had squawked. Even more frustrating, however, was his expression, which clearly said that he regretted what had just transpired between them. She wanted to grab him by the lapels and shake him until he realized that he couldn't keep running away from her.

"Sorry, but if Vivian's paging, it must be urgent."

He turned to leave, but then stopped and faced her again. "By the way, I don't participate in orgies. I have never bowled in my life. I play a decent game of golf, and I abhor boxing. I am, however, an excellent marathon runner, and once a year I—" His speech was interrupted by another page from Vivian, and he gave a fatalistic shrug. "It's definitely urgent. See you later."

"Just what do you do once a year?" Christy murmured as she watched him walk away with a stride that was sexy as all get out. It was then that she admitted that she was more than infatuated with him; she was downright besotted.

The trouble was, Adam seemed resolute about ignoring the chemistry between them. Consequently she was in a muddle over what she should do about it. He wasn't the type of man she was accustomed to dealing with, so she wasn't sure how to handle him. He was so reserved that she feared she'd scare him off if she came on too strong. Yet, if she didn't come on strong enough, she probably wouldn't make it to first base.

She shook her head in frustration, realizing she was late for work. Her father would be waiting for her, probably grumbling and pacing, so she would have to think about Adam later. And she had every intention of giving him considerable thought. She'd never felt this exhilarating excitement over a man. Though it could blow up in her face, Adam was most assuredly worth the risk.

CHRISTY AND HER FATHER were enjoying another lull in business. She sat on the stool behind her camera, pretending to listen to her father's rambling conversation while she thought about Adam.

She still couldn't figure out exactly why she was so attracted to him, though she did know that it didn't stem from a lack of male companionship. Gregarious by nature, she dated frequently. But since having helped nurse her father back to health these past months, she longed for a more meaningful relationship. Was that what was happening here? Did she see in Adam an answer to that need?

It made sense. He was older and, therefore, more stable than most of the men she dated. He knew exactly what he wanted out of life. He'd had plenty of time to sow his oats, and—

"Santa to elf," Robert announced, waving his hand in front of Christy's face, bringing her out of her reverie.

She gave him a guilty smile. "I'm sorry, Pop. My mind was wandering."

"You looked as if you'd lost it altogether. Are you all right?"

"I'm fine," she assured, hearing the worry in his voice. "I was just thinking about Adam Worth."

"Scrooge?" he asked in surprise. "Why? Is something wrong?"

"Nothing's wrong, Pop. He's just different, isn't he?"

"He's a classic type-A personality," Robert stated, bracing his elbows against the railing. "All he knows is work, work and more work. In about ten years, he'll have a nervous breakdown or a heart attack. If he survives, he'll take about five minutes to smell the roses before he throws himself back into the grind."

"Pop, that's an awful thing to say!" Christy chastised.

He shrugged. "It's the truth. I've seen his kind before. They're driven, and nothing can slow them down. They spend their life trying to succeed, and then go to their grave without ever enjoying that success."

The thought of Adam facing such a fate saddened Christy. "But surely that type of personality can be reformed?"

Robert regarded her suspiciously. "Why would you want to reform him?"

She blushed and looked away, not ready to reveal her feelings for Adam. "I haven't fulfilled my quota of good deeds for the year."

"Christmas, Adam Worth is a hopeless cause. Don't get tangled up with him. You'll only get hurt."

"I'm not going to get tangled up with him!" she said impatiently. She loved her father, but she hated his propensity to hover over her as if she were a little girl needing protection. "I would just like to see Adam relax and have some fun."

Before Robert could offer more objections, a flood of children arrived, and Christy was saved. It was either feast or famine in the Santa-picture business, and she hoped that this tidal wave would last long enough to divert her father's attention. She wasn't ready for a lecture, particularly when she'd already planned to reform Adam Worth. She rubbed her hands together in anticipation as she returned to her camera and began considering ways she could accomplish her mission.

3

FEELING RESTLESS and oddly out of sync, Adam prowled through the mall. It wasn't the first time he'd experienced these feelings, but it was the first time that work hadn't eased them.

He approached the North Pole booth, acknowledging that his restlessness was connected with Christy Knight. She made him laugh and made him feel calm when his world was topsy-turvy. He also desired her, and that scared the hell out of him.

When he reached the North Pole booth, he scanned it, searching for Christy. His desire to see her was so strong that he felt he could conjure her up. Since the Knights weren't due for another hour, he stepped inside the railed area and sat down in the chair. What would it be like to play Santa Claus? It was almost impossible to imagine, considering that he'd never actually had a chance to believe in the jolly old man.

Resting his head against the chair, he sighed. He'd never forget the day when he was five years old and his father, who'd just been laid off from work, told him he couldn't afford to buy him any presents, and that there was no Santa Claus. His mother was furious over his father's revelation and filed for divorce because of it.

Well, that wasn't exactly true, Adam conceded. The divorce had been the result of many problems, but his father's announcement had been the proverbial straw that broke the camel's back. From that moment on, the Christmas holidays had become a battleground.

He shook his head, recalling how, whenever the holidays approached, his mother had complained to him about the pittance she received for child support, while his young stepmother railed that child support was putting his father on the brink of bankruptcy. He'd felt so damn guilty whenever he opened the meager packages under the tree. But he had to admit that he'd learned a hard lesson from his miserable childhood Christmases. Financial success was the key to happiness, and he'd gotten a college education to ensure that he never suffered his father's plight.

As the familiar depression that always hit him at this time of year returned, he pushed the painful memories back into the past. Then he closed his eyes and allowed himself to fantasize how it would be to sit in this chair and have a bright-eyed little girl or boy crawl up on his knee to confide their secret Christmas wishes.

He was so lost in the fantasy that his eyes flew open in shock when a voice drawled, "You look good in that chair."

Adam gave Christy a guilty look as he hurriedly got up. "I, uh, was waiting for someone," he said. "They're late. I guess they aren't coming."

Knowing he was lying, Christy regarded him curiously. He looked positively panic-stricken—a definite overreaction.

"Since your appointment is late, why don't you join me for a breakfast croissant at Croissant City?" she suggested. She'd already eaten, but it was the first opportunity she'd had to get Adam alone for more than a minute, and she wasn't about to let it pass her by.

Adam's first impulse was to refuse her invitation. She'd just caught him sitting in Santa's chair, and he half believed she had intuited his ridiculous daydream. He knew he was being irrational, which, like his depression, was another personality quirk that tended to resurface at this time of year.

"Sure," he agreed, going toward her and taking her elbow.

Christy felt his touch right down to her toes, and it affected her so powerfully, she was unable to speak. They walked the length of the mall in silence, and when they reached their destination, she stared in indecision at the overhead menu that listed fifty varieties of croissants.

"I don't know why I come here," she confided to Adam. "They all sound so good that I can never make up my mind. I always end up at McDonald's restaurant."

"Then you should do what I do. Go down the list alphabetically. That way, you can try them all and discover which are your favorites."

"Do you approach everything so systematically?" she inquired.

"Usually," he answered. Had he become that predictable? The question disturbed him, because he suddenly wondered if he'd fallen into a rut.

"You never do anything spontaneous?" she asked next.

"Rarely," he replied, recalling the many unplanned visits he'd made to the North Pole booth. Did those count as spontaneous acts? "Whenever I've done something impulsive, it's usually gotten me into trouble."

"What kind of trouble?"

He chuckled at her smile. "Nothing you'd be interested in. Are you going to try my system?"

But she was interested in everything about him. "I'll try your system. Since I've never done anything systematic in my life, it'll be a new experience."

Adam ordered an apple croissant for Christy and a date one for himself. They carried their food and steaming cups of coffee to one of the small booths that faced the corridor.

"What made you open a mall?" she asked after taking a bite of her croissant, liking the tart apple flavor almost as much as looking at Adam.

"I'm afraid that's a long and boring story," he answered.

He was avoiding the question—just as he'd avoided the one about the trouble he'd gotten into when he'd been impulsive. When had he come to the conclusion that people wouldn't be interested in what he'd done? Christy suspected that that was his rationale. "I have forty-five minutes before I have to go to work, and my coffee will keep me awake."

"You're sure you're interested?" he asked doubtfully.

"Absolutely. After all, how many mall owners does one meet in one's lifetime?"

"I've met quite a few."

"You're an oddity."

Her smile softened the description, but Adam wondered if she'd meant it in more ways than one. He circled the rim of his plastic cup with his finger. What should he tell her? Really, it was a long and boring story. Yet, for some inexplicable reason, he wanted to share it with her.

"My father is a construction worker. When I was twelve, he was working for a building contractor who made the steel frames for commercial and industrial buildings. They had a contract on a mall near my school, and I'd have lunch with him. One day the mall's owner visited the site. Dad's boss introduced us, and Harlan took a liking to me. He told me to stop by the office when the mall opened and he'd see if he couldn't find me something to do for pocket money."

"And that was the beginning of all this?"

"Basically. Harlan gave me a job. I worked for him through high school and during summers while I went to college. When I graduated from college, he offered me an assistant manager's job at a mall he'd just opened in Albuquerque. From there, I ended up as manager at his mall in Phoenix, and then at another one in St. Louis. Somewhere along the line, I decided that I wanted to own my own mall and began saving for it."

He didn't bother to explain that the "somewhere along the line" had been his engagement to Andrea. But her life-style hadn't meshed with his, and she'd eventually walked out. Fortunately, she'd done so before they'd married. Still, it had hurt like hell, and he'd thrown himself back into his work to get over her. Now he was realizing his dream, and he didn't have anyone to share it with. It was damn depressing.

Christy, noticing Adam drift away from her, brought him back by asking, "How did your employer take the news that you were going to be his competition?"

Adam smiled. "Harlan didn't mind. He's no longer expanding, and he offered to be my cosignatory."

Christy, impressed by the revelation, let out a low whistle. That kind of offer showed a deep trust. "He must like you very much."

Adam shrugged. "I never thought about it that way, but I guess he must."

Christy didn't comment. As she sipped her coffee, she speculated why such a handsome, self-possessed man would look so surprised by the notion that his old boss liked him. It conveyed a sense of vulnerability that didn't fit with the confident, successful image Adam presented to the world. Christy began to suspect that a good portion of that image was worn as a suit of armor to protect himself.

What was it that had hurt him so badly? Or maybe the question should be, *Who* had hurt him so badly? A woman? She didn't like the thought of him being that emotionally connected to a woman, though she knew she was being foolish. Adam was thirty-seven years old. Somewhere along the line he would have fallen victim to Cupid's arrows.

"What made you go into photography?" he suddenly asked.

This time Christy shrugged. "Mom and Pop were in their forties when I came along, and they were so thrilled at finally having a baby that they were forever taking pictures of me. Since I grew up in front of a camera, it seemed natural for me to get behind one."

"You're very talented at it," he stated sincerely.

"I know," she said without a trace of arrogance. "But the best part of my career is that it fulfills me. Does running your mall fulfill you?"

Her question disturbed Adam, because he wanted to give her a resounding "Yes." Instead, he discovered that it wasn't nearly so fulfilling as it was the only thing he knew how to do.

"I suppose it does," he replied. It was time to end the conversation. Christy was raising too many questions he didn't have answers for, and Adam had learned long ago that all that self-analysis accomplished was a state of frustration. He had enough frustrations in his life right now. "I have a million things to do, Christy, so I'd better get going. I'll see you later."

"Yeah. Later," Christy responded. This scenario was becoming darned aggravating—each time she began to learn something about him, he took off.

It was going to take time to get close to him. Fortunately she'd been blessed with an overabundance of patience. When it came to Adam, she had the feeling she was going to be using every ounce of it.

IT WAS LATE AFTERNOON before Adam returned to the "North Pole." Having been caught in Santa's chair had made him shy away from the booth. He'd resolved to avoid it for the remainder of the day, but he eventually found himself walking in that direction. After all, what kind of trouble could he get into by spontaneously visiting the Knights?

Robert was sitting in his chair, tapping his foot and scowling at his daughter, who was in deep conversation with a young boy. The boy's arms were crossed over his chest and his expression was mutinous. Behind him was a long line of glaring parents with restless children.

"Have a problem?" he asked.

Christy glanced up at him, her expression harried. "Yes. Tommy says he's too old to have his picture taken with Santa."

Adam's gaze drifted over the child, who couldn't have been more than six—maybe seven if he was small for his age. "Then I suppose he is."

"Oh, come on, Adam," Christy muttered as she took his arm and led him a short distance away. After making sure that Tommy couldn't hear them, she said, "He's a little boy, so don't encourage him."

"Sometimes little boys like to think they're big boys. And who's to say they're not? Age doesn't necessarily dictate maturity."

"Adam, look over my shoulder and you'll see his mother. She's a sweet woman with three toddlers, all of whom have had their picture taken with Santa. She wants Tommy to have his picture taken, too."

"Why doesn't she tell him that?"

"She has, but he's stubborn. Even Pop couldn't convince him."

"Then I suggest that Tommy's mother bring him back another day. You have other customers waiting. By the glares they're directing at you, I think they're considering hanging both you and Tommy."

Christy let out a resigned sigh. "I suppose you're right, but Pop and I have had such good luck with the kids so far. I'm afraid that if we let Tommy have his way, it's going to start a run of bad luck."

"That's a little superstitious, isn't it?"

"I'm a very superstitious person, and my instincts say that if I let Tommy get away with this, I'm going to regret it."

Adam gave her shoulder a reassuring squeeze. "Well, as much as I have faith in your instincts, I also see that you have some very disgruntled customers. If you don't start waiting on them, your run of bad luck is going to start—with or without Tommy."

Christy acknowledged the truth of his words—even though she didn't want to. "Yeah. I guess I'll just have to tell Tommy's mother to bring him back another time."

As Christy walked away, her shoulders slumped in dejection. Adam frowned. He glanced from her to the boy causing her distress. The least he could do was try to help.

"Christy?" When she turned to look at him, he said, "Bring Tommy over here. I'll see if I can't persuade him to have his picture taken."

"You?" she questioned doubtfully.

"You don't have to sound so skeptical," he grumbled. "I happen to have a way with children. My mother says it's a knack."

She still looked skeptical, but nevertheless brought Tommy to him. Adam reached down and lifted the boy over the railing. Tommy regarded him suspiciously when he set him on his feet. "Why don't you get back to work?" Adam advised Christy.

"Sure," she said, but seemed hesitant about leaving him alone with Tommy. Then she shrugged and went back to her camera.

Once Christy was hard at work with her next customers, Adam placed a foot on the railing and rested his elbow on his knee. Peering down at the boy, he said, "I understand you're too old to have your picture taken with Santa, Tommy."

"Yeah. Only babies do that kinda stuff. I'm not a baby," Tommy informed him with a defiant lift of his chin.

Adam, remembering his own sentiments at the same age, nodded in agreement. "I know how it is, but your mother wants you to have your picture taken. Don't you think you can make an exception this time and do it for her?"

"Nope," the boy said, recrossing his arms over his chest.

"Why not? I bet she does things for you that she doesn't want to do."

"Like what?"

"Bake cookies?" Adam guessed, remembering that his mother had hated baking cookies.

Tommy shook his head. "Naw. She likes to do that. She said so."

It was evident Tommy hadn't lived long enough for guilt to be used as an adequate weapon. Trying another tactic, Adam asked, "Are your friends having their pictures taken with Santa?"

"Only the sissies. The rest of us know that their ain't no Santa Claus."

Despite the bravado with which Tommy had made the announcement, Adam saw the look of disappointment in his eyes. Recalling his own childhood, he felt a surge of anger that someone had caused the same disillusionment he'd experienced himself as a child.

"Who told you that?" When Tommy's head shot up, and his lower lip trembled, Adam saw he'd asked the question too sharply.

"Brian."

"Who's Brian?" he asked, softening his voice.

"My best friend."

"And what makes him such an expert on Santa Claus?"

"His big brother told him all about it. He said that all you have to do is sneak around the house and you'll find all your presents. Santa doesn't bring them. Your mommy and daddy bring them."

The tone of Tommy's voice made it quite clear that he considered Brian's and his older brother's words gospel. "Well, I hate to tell you this, pal, but Brian and his brother are wrong."

"Oh, yeah? Says who?" Tommy challenged.

"Says me," Adam answered. "It's true that you can sometimes find your presents, but that's because there are so many girls and boys in the world today. Santa's reindeer are getting too old to carry all that loot in one trip, so they make some early trips. Then Santa flies in on Christmas Eve, gets your presents from your parents, and sticks them under the tree."

"Oh, yeah?" Tommy repeated. This time, he didn't sound belligerent but hopeful.

"Yep."

"Then that guy is really Santa Claus?"

Adam followed Tommy's gaze to Robert Knight who was cuddling up to an adorable little girl with apple-red cheeks.

"He sure is," Adam said.

"I don't believe you."

"Why not?"

"Because I've seen a whole bunch of Santas, and Brian says they're all fakes. He says if you pull their beard, it comes right off."

"Well, Brian is wrong again. Some of those Santas are just helpers, but our Santa is the real one. His beard doesn't come off, because it's just as real as he is."

Tommy placed his hands on the next-to-the-top rail and stuck his head closer to the opening so he could study Robert Knight. "It does look real."

"It is. When you have your picture taken, you can give it a tug—a gentle one," Adam added, "and you'll see I'm right."

"I don't know. Even if he is real, I'm too old to have my picture taken with him."

Adam sighed. They'd come so far, only to end up where they'd started. "You're not too old, Tommy. In fact, I'm not too old."

The moment Adam made the statement, he regretted it. Tommy was staring at him assessingly, and Adam guessed what the boy was going to say.

"I'll have my picture taken if you do."

Adam cast a glance at Robert Knight, then at the waiting crowd. He'd never had his picture taken with Santa Claus, and he wasn't going to start now—particularly when it would be witnessed by what appeared to be half the population of Colorado Springs.

"I can't do that, Tommy. It wouldn't be fair. All these people have been waiting in line. I'd be crowding in, and they'd get mad at me."

For a moment, he thought he'd outmaneuvered the boy, but then Tommy responded, "That's all right. I'll tell them that I saved your place for you."

"How's everything going?" Christy asked before Adam could think of another argument.

Tommy pointed at Adam and said, "He's going to have his picture taken with Santa. Then I'll have mine taken."

"That sounds like a great idea," Christy exclaimed, grinning at Adam's stormy expression. "Why don't you go tell your mom so she can comb your hair?" When Tommy ran off to comply, she added, "That was a great psychological move. I'm proud of you, Adam."

"I'm not going to have my picture taken," he declared irritably.

"Sure, you are." She took his arm and led him around the edge of the railing and through the opening. "You promised Tommy. Besides, you should have a picture to commemorate the mall's first Christmas. Now, go stand by Santa and smile. We'll have your picture taken in two shakes of a reindeer's tail."

Adam glared at her, but there was no graceful way out. He'd just persuaded a kid to switch his allegiance from his best friend, who'd told the truth, to him, who'd told a lie. He didn't regret restoring Tommy's faith in Santa Claus, but he vowed that he'd never come near the North Pole booth again.

He turned to approach Robert Knight, but stopped when Christy teasingly reminded, "Oh, by the way, Adam, don't forget to tell Santa what a good little boy you've been so he'll be sure to give you what you want for Christmas."

The entire crowd chuckled, and he gave her a look that should have turned her into a pillar of salt. He went over to Robert Knight, who stood and put his arm around Adam's shoulder. Even telling himself that Christy was right—that he should have a picture to commemorate the mall's first Christmas—didn't cool his flaring temper, because Adam suddenly felt five years old again, and he could see his father's defeated expression as his mother screamed at him.

To his horror, Robert jumped right into the game, entertaining the crowd by insisting on carrying out his entire routine of, "What's your name, little boy? Have you been good this year? Tell Santa what you want for Christmas."

Adam decided that he deserved an Academy Award as he played along with Robert, because his temper was rising by the minute, though he wasn't angry with the older man. It was just that all the old resentments over his miserable holidays past were reviving. No matter how hard he tried to suppress them, he couldn't. All he'd ever wanted was one happy Christmas. Just *one*. Had that really been too much to ask for?

When Christy told him to smile, Adam complied. With self-control he'd never known he possessed, he left the booth, pausing long enough to shake hands with Tommy's mother and a few other customers. He even managed a polite "No problem," when Christy thanked him for his help. Pleading lateness for an appointment, he then rushed off.

Christy approached her father with a nervous smile. "I think we overplayed it. He's furious."

"He'll survive," Robert said complacently.

"I'm not so sure about that," she replied, gnawing on her bottom lip as she stared down the corridor Adam had taken. She knew her father had purposely deviled him. She also knew that they'd somehow hurt Adam.

While considering whether to go after Adam and apologize, Christy heard, "Hey, are you going to take my picture?"

Christy observed that Tommy now appeared to be as eager to have his picture taken with Santa as he'd been determined not to earlier.

"Sure," Christy said, planning to apologize to Adam later. "Hop up on Santa's lap."

"Ouch!" Robert yelped as Tommy, who'd scrambled onto his lap, gave his beard a hearty tug.

"It *is* real!" the boy exclaimed in delight. "That man was right. You are the real Santa Claus!"

"Of course he is!" Christy returned before Robert could grumble a complaint. "Now smile, Tommy, so we can take your picture."

"Not until I've told Santa what I want for Christmas, and I have a *really* big list."

Robert groaned, Christy smiled, and Tommy began to babble.

IT WAS LATE EVENING when Christy knocked on Adam's office door. There was no answer, so she jiggled the doorknob. Finding the door unlocked, she entered. Adam's secretary had obviously gone home for the day since her typewriter was covered.

The door to his private office was open, and she headed for it, calling, "Adam, are you here?"

She heard his muffled curse and stepped through the doorway just in time to see him hurriedly snap the elastic of a pair of sweatpants into place at his waist.

"What are you doing here?" Adam demanded, his voice brusque at almost being caught with his pants down—or, to be more accurate, off.

"I'm looking for you," Christy replied, as a blush rose to her cheeks at the sight of his half-naked body. She knew she should apologize for bursting in on him and leave, but she was unable to tear her gaze from his bare chest, let alone make her legs move. He was well muscled, with a light dusting of hair across his chest that narrowed into a fine line and trailed seductively to his trim waist. A warm fluttering came to life low in her abdomen. She'd known Adam was magnificent, but she hadn't realized he was one of those men who was even better-looking with his clothes off. She found herself entertaining the naughty wish that he hadn't had time to get his pants on before she'd walked into the room.

Adam, well aware of the direction of Christy's scrutiny, felt an intense surge of desire erupt. He was tempted to cross the room, sweep her into his arms, and see if she was ready to fulfill the sensual promise he saw reflected in her eyes. But if he issued the challenge and she accepted it, he'd be in for trouble. Christy wasn't a woman a man dallied with, and dalliance was all he had time for at this point in his overworked life. He reached for his sweatshirt.

Christy had to bite her tongue to keep from asking Adam to leave it off. Instead she asked, "Going for a run?"

"Yeah." He pulled the sweatshirt over his head. "Did you need something?"

"I wanted to apologize," she said, clasping her hands tightly together in front of her. Her fingers were begging to smooth his disheveled hair or, better yet, to muss it up even more. "Pop and I were pretty hard on you this afternoon, and it wasn't fair. You saved the day, and all we did was tease you."

Adam sat in his chair and began to put on his socks. "Your apology is accepted, but unnecessary. I didn't mind the teasing. As you said, I should have a picture to commemorate the mall's first Christmas. Anything else?"

The very fact that he refused to look at her told Christy he was lying. She still didn't understand exactly how she and her father had hurt him, but she could sense his pain and wanted to comfort him somehow. She wanted to tell him there was no need to hide behind a polite facade with her—that he could let his feelings out.

But she suspected he wouldn't be open to such a suggestion. Obviously, he had been hiding his feelings for years—a habit that would be hard to break. This meant that there was only one way she could reach him. And she *needed* to reach him—she couldn't bear the thought that he was hurting over something she'd done, even if it had been unintentional.

She drew in a deep breath for courage and said, "Yes, there is something else. Will you kiss me?"

Adam froze. One look at her face confirmed that his hearing hadn't failed him.

Everything inside him told him to spring up out of his chair and haul her into his arms before she changed her mind. Instead, he finished putting on his socks. "I don't think that would be a good idea."

"Why not?" Christy asked as she rounded his desk and stood directly in front of him. "Is it because you think you're too old for me?"

"That's part of it." He leaned back in his chair and stared at her somberly. "Twelve years is a hell of an age difference. I probably graduated from high school before you started first grade."

"Probably," Christy conceded as she sat on the edge of his desk. "But I've been out of first grade for a long time, Adam."

When she started to swing her legs, Adam's gaze was drawn to them automatically. "Why are you pursuing this, Christy?"

She gave a wry smile. "At least you're acknowledging that there's a 'this' to pursue." When Adam didn't respond, she said, "I like you, Adam, and I think you like me. Would it be so wrong for us to date and get to know each other?"

"Yes, it would be wrong," he responded firmly. "Christy, you're lovely and vibrant, and ... young. You need someone who can share your enthusiasm for life. I can't—I'm just too cynical. And even if I wasn't, I simply don't have room in my life for a relationship. The mall takes up every moment of my time. Hell, I don't even have time to sleep. It's only going to get worse before it gets better. Do you understand what I'm saying?"

"Oh, I understand," she stated dryly, "but I think you're using our age difference and the mall as excuses to avoid seeing me. Why, Adam? Do you find me childish? Am I unattractive to you?"

Adam raked a hand impatiently through his hair at her puzzled expression. If she'd been angry or hurt, he would have known how to deal with her. How was he supposed to respond to puzzlement? "No, I don't find you childish, and I think you're damned attractive."

"So, what's the problem?" she asked.

"I told you. I don't have time for you in my life right now, so let's just drop the subject."

Christy watched his face settle into a closed expression. Her father claimed Adam was a type-A personality, but she disagreed. She believed that Adam was running from something—and that it was easier for him to immerse himself in work than it was to commit himself to living. But she wasn't going to let him get away with it. Her father's heart attack had taught her that life was too short to sit back and let it pass you by. She was determined to teach Adam how to live—even if he ended up hating her for it.

She slid off his desk, put a hand on each arm of his chair and leaned forward so that her eyes were level with his. "Be honest with me, Adam. You don't have the time to see me? Or you don't want to *make* the time to see me?"

"Both," he answered as he raised his chin and met her gaze head-on. "I don't have the time, Christy. Even if I did, I still wouldn't date you."

"Because you're too old for me?" When he didn't reply, Christy said, "You're using my age as a smoke screen, Adam. Rumor has it that you're a workaholic, and I think that you're refusing to go out with me because you've forgotten how to have fun."

"That's ridiculous," he muttered irritably.

"Then prove it to me," she taunted.

"And how am I supposed to do that?" he snapped.

She gave him a smug smile. "A man who knows how to have a good time wouldn't have to ask that question." When he glowered at her, she said, "Kiss me, Adam. Prove to me that the man who exists inside those three-piece suits knows how to let loose. Show me that he knows how to live. Make me believe that he has blood running through his veins instead of accounting ledgers and computer printouts."

Christy had just flung the one arrow guaranteed to hit Adam's most sensitive spot. Andrea had made similar accusations the day she'd thrown Adam's engagement ring at him and stormed out of his office.

Adam was furious with Christy for making him sound as if he were a machine. Before he even knew what he was doing, he caught the back of her head in his hand and drew her face toward him. If she wanted him to prove he had blood in his veins, then, by damn, he'd prove it!

He had every intention of giving her a crushing kiss, but just before her eyes fluttered closed in surrender, he saw the trust in their depths. His anger dissolved, and he told himself he should throw her out of his office before he did something he'd regret. But she parted her lips invitingly, and as he gazed at them, he knew he was lost.

He told himself he was crazy as he brushed his lips over hers, reveling at the sigh that vibrated in the back of her throat, causing his blood to run hot and his body to tremble.

Pull away before it's too late! his conscience screamed at him. But Christy chose that moment to deepen the kiss, and Adam knew he was in serious trouble.

He groaned as he pulled her onto his lap and let himself flow with her kiss. For once, the word *Christmas* might mean something worth looking forward to.

4

CHRISTY'S MIND SHUT DOWN as Adam pulled her onto his lap. His lips settled against hers in a gentle, brushing motion that was more devastating to her senses than any passionate kiss she'd ever shared.

A small moan of desire escaped her when his tongue teased for entrance into her mouth. She wrapped her arms around his neck, arching against him as she parted her lips. His tongue made an intimate tour of her mouth, One of his hands cradled the back of her head and the other rested lightly in the curve of her waist. She buried her fingers in his hair and tried to get even closer to him.

Christy felt so right in Adam's arms, and when she arched against him and parted her lips invitingly, he thought he'd explode. He would have liked to throw her down on the floor and make passionate love to her, but he couldn't bring himself to move for fear of breaking the magical spell she'd woven around him. Instead, he kissed her experimentally, absorbing the alluring texture of her lips, until he could no longer ignore the need to explore further.

Slowly, he entered her mouth, and the taste of her was so arousing it made him shudder. When her tongue met his, his self-protective instincts began to clamor. She was more bewitching than he'd imagined. He couldn't afford to let the kiss continue; neither could he bring himself to leave her abruptly. Withdrawing from her was the most exquisite torture he'd ever endured.

"More," Christy mumbled as Adam drew away, leaving her feeling breathless and unfulfilled.

He chuckled and dropped a quick kiss on the tip of her nose. "Don't be greedy."

She pressed her head against his shoulder and gazed up at him. "I want to be greedy. Kiss me again."

Adam brushed his knuckles against her cheek, marveling at the silken smoothness of her skin. He was sorely tempted to obey her request, but if he did, he mightn't be able to stop with just a kiss.

"You're incorrigible," he teased.

She grinned. "I know. Now, kiss me again."

Adam shook his head reluctantly and eased her off his lap. "Any more kissing and all my courtly manners will fly out the window."

Christy wanted to tell him to forget his courtly manners, but such a declaration would be too rash. So far, all she'd managed to do was make Adam angry enough to kiss her. Now she was going to have to compel him to date her, and that might not be such an easy task.

She sat on the edge of his desk, studying his controlled expression and wishing she could read his mind.

"Why are you staring at me?" he asked after she'd been silent for a long time.

"I'm just thinking that you're a better kisser than I'd imagined. I can't wait for a repeat performance," she responded bluntly.

"Christy, stop it," Adam muttered as he closed his eyes and fought the desire stirring inside him. It seemed as if every time he steeled himself against her, she managed to find a chink in his armor. He could have handled flirtation or coyness, but her honesty was as arousing as it was unnerving.

"Don't ask questions if you don't want to hear the truth," she stated softly.

He opened his eyes and frowned at her. "I'm a workaholic, remember? That means that I'm no good for you."

"Too much chocolate isn't any good for me, either, but I overindulge in it, anyway," she replied. She braced her hands on the edge of his desk and leaned toward him as she said, "All I'm asking for is some time to get to know you, Adam. The worst that can happen is that we'll end up walking away from each other. We could become good friends, and a person can never have too many friends. What do you say?"

Adam propped his elbow on the arm of his chair and rested his chin on his hand as he studied her. Was she suggesting that they try to be friends after the kiss they'd just shared? She couldn't possibly be so naive.

"If I did agree to see you, I wouldn't be looking for friendship," he answered equally bluntly. "I'd want to be your lover. Are you ready to deal with that? Do you understand the consequences if it doesn't work out? Have you ever lived through a failed love affair?"

"There's no such thing as a failed love affair," she countered. "If you care enough to make love with someone, then you gain something from the experience."

"You sure as hell do," he ruefully agreed. "You learn how it feels to have your heart broken."

"That's true, but you also learn how to live. And even if it ends up in heartache, it's better than not living at all."

"I don't know, Christy." He looked perplexed. "A part of me says I should pat you on the head and send you on your way."

"And what does the other part say?" she prompted.

He gave her a mirthless smile. "It says I should say to hell with chivalry and take advantage of what you're offering."

"I see." She slid off his desk. "Well, when you decide which part you want to listen to, you know where I'm at."

She moved toward the door and glanced over her shoulder at him. "By the way, Adam, while you're wrestling with your conscience, don't try to take the easy way out by doing what you think is best for me. I'm the only person who can make that decision, and I've already decided that you're worth taking a chance on."

With that, she left, leaving Adam gazing at the empty doorway in exasperation.

She'd done it again! Why didn't she respond the way he expected her to? He'd planned on her giving him an argument. If she'd argued with him, he'd have been able to maintain his position, because he was a master debater. But she hadn't argued, and he was floundering.

He angrily batted at a pile of papers on his desk, sending them scattering across the floor. He wasn't going to get involved with her, because—

"Oh, damn!" he exclaimed under his breath when he realized that he was searching for excuses to keep from getting involved with Christy. It was time he was honest with himself. She was right. It wasn't her age or the mall that was worrying him; the truth was, he was *afraid* to get involved with her.

Frowning in irritation with himself, he leaned back in his chair. Ever since Andrea had walked out on him, he'd avoided anything more than a casual relationship, because he feared he'd fail again, and he wasn't accustomed to failure. Success had become his mantra.

He rose to his feet and walked to the window. As he stared out at the lighted parking lot, he conjured up the image of Christy sitting on his desk and telling him that there was no such thing as a failed love affair. And what was it she'd said? Something like, "You learn how to live. Even if it ends up in heartache, it's better than not living at all."

Adam admitted that for several years now, he hadn't been living at all. So, what was he going to do about it? Go after Christy? At least he'd be living, failure or not.

Turning away from the window, he strode purposefully through his office and into Vivian's. He was so focused on what he was going to say to Christy, he gasped when a feminine voice drawled, "Looking for someone?"

He spun around and shook his head in disbelief when he spied Christy sitting in Vivian's chair, her hands folded behind her head and her feet propped up on the desk.

"What are you doing here?" he asked warily.

"Waiting for you to come after me, of course," she said with a cheeky grin. "What took you so long? I'm starving. If you don't feed me soon, I may fade away right before your eyes."

Adam burst into roaring laughter at her audacity, rounded the desk and hauled her into his arms, treating her to another devastating kiss that made Christy even more ravenous—but not for food.

"SO, WHEN ARE WE GOING out on our first date?" Christy asked as she stole her sixth fried mushroom from Adam's plate. They were eating at a small family restaurant in the mall since he was dressed in his jogging clothes and she still wore her elf costume.

Adam playfully swatted at her hand. "You said you didn't want mushrooms, so leave mine alone. And we're on our first date."

"This isn't a date," Christy revised as she popped the mushroom into her mouth. "It's a celebration in honor of you exercising your good sense."

"You're impossible," he replied with a wry laugh.

"So I've been told. Now, when are we going out?"

Adam became pensive. "I don't know, Christy. I'm swamped right now. Until I can find a manager, I won't have much time to devote to you."

"I don't need a lot of time, Adam. A few hours here and there will satisfy me, for now."

He caught her hand and brushed his thumb across her knuckles, trembling inside as he felt a tiny shiver rush through her fingers. For the first time in his life, he wanted to say to hell with work and responsibility, and drag her off to some remote place where he could devote twenty-four hours a day to her.

"Are you always so agreeable?" he inquired, concerned by how quickly things were moving between them. All they'd actually shared were a few conversations and two kisses, and he was already obsessed with her. If he wasn't careful, he was going to find himself in over his head.

"No, but I am reasonable," she replied, lacing her fingers with his. She still couldn't believe Adam had capitulated so easily, and was so relieved he had that she'd been counting her blessings all through dinner. "I know you're busy. All I ask is that you set aside a little time for me."

"You're busy, too," he pointed out. "After all, you're developing photographs after you leave here. Why don't you look at your schedule and come up with some times that are convenient for you? Unless I have a pressing commitment, I'll take time off."

"Even if it's in the middle of a workday?" she asked.

Her tone had been too casual and Adam regarded her suspiciously. "I don't know. Why?"

"Because Pop and I have Tuesdays off. How would you like to go sledding with me on Tuesday afternoon?"

"You want *me* to go sledding?"

Christy would have laughed at his astonished look, but she feared he might think she was making fun of him. "Why not? We'd get plenty of fresh air and sunshine. You could have three or four hours with no phones, no crowds and no problems. It would be just you, me and a sled on a deserted hill in the middle of nowhere."

Adam did have to admit that the idea of no phones, no crowds and no problems was appealing, but sledding? It sounded so . . . young. To his surprise, however, that made it even more appealing. It had been ages since he'd done something completely out of character.

"I really would like to go, Christy, but I'd have to leave Vivian in charge, and too many problems can arise for one person to handle. Until I can find a manager, I can't afford to be completely cut off from the office."

Christy could tell by his expression that he wasn't just making up the excuse. Adam really needed a break from the mall—there were lines of tension etched around his eyes and mouth. She'd suggested sledding because he'd told her he was a runner, which meant he must enjoy outdoor activity. Nothing was more relaxing than a good romp in the snow.

But she had to agree that it wouldn't be right to leave Vivian alone. Adam handled everything from shoplifting to accidents to maintenance problems on a daily basis. She was ready to concede defeat when Bertha

Gonzales walked by the restaurant, spied them through the window and waved.

"I'll be right back," Christy explained as she slid out of the booth. "Don't move a muscle."

Adam gave an amused shake of his head as she raced out of the restaurant, her elf cap bouncing precariously. As he sipped his coffee, he wondered what she was up to as he watched her catch up with Bertha and engage her in animated conversation.

A few moments later, she slid back into the booth and gave him a triumphant smile. "I just solved your problem. Bertha said that her daughter would be happy to help Vivian out for an afternoon. So you can take a few hours off."

"I don't know," Adam responded uncertainly.

"Adam, you definitely need to expand your vocabulary. If you say 'I don't know' one more time, I'm going to bop you over the head with something. And why don't you know? Suzanne spends half her life in Vivian's office, anyway. Bertha says you won't even have to pay her, because she'll pay *you* to take Suzanne off her hands for an afternoon."

"Well, of course I'll pay her," he muttered. "I wouldn't expect the girl to work for nothing."

"Then you'll go?" Christy asked excitedly.

Adam should say no. Even with help in the office, he'd be dumping a lot of responsibility on Vivian. Of course, she'd have Security and Maintenance to help her, and the paramedics and the police were only a phone call away. It wouldn't be as if he were leaving her all alone, and it was only for one afternoon.

"Assuming that Vivian has no objections, and assuming that I don't have any appointments that can't be rescheduled, I'll go," he said.

"It's a deal." She grinned in satisfaction. Then she glanced at her watch and gave him a resigned look. "I need to get home. I have a ton of film to develop."

"It was a busy day?"

"Yes, but I'm not complaining. The more money I make, the more solvent I become, and that makes my mortgage company happy."

"I know the feeling well," Adam replied, signaling the waitress for the bill.

When they left the restaurant, Adam draped his arm around Christy's shoulders, and she slipped her arm around his waist and sighed in contentment. She had fantasized about what it would be like to walk with him like this, but she hadn't imagined that it would feel so right.

"Where's your coat?" Adam asked when they reached the doors leading to the parking lot.

"In the car," Christy answered. She smiled when his lips settled into a disapproving line. "It's a short dash, Adam, and since you don't have your coat, we'd better say goodbye here."

"I'm not letting you walk to your car alone in the dark," he objected.

"I've been doing it ever since I came to work here," she informed him. "And I take precautions. I'm parked under the third streetlight. You can stand here and watch until I'm safely inside." She steered him away from the doors and behind a large potted palm that stood in the corner. "Now, give me a good-night kiss. If you make it an extra-special one, it might last me until morning."

After checking to make sure the area was empty, Adam leaned against the wall and drew her between his thighs. "What are people going to think if they see me kissing an elf?"

"That you're bribing me so that I'll make sure Santa gives you what you want for Christmas?" she suggested.

He chuckled. "You're so damn quick with a comeback."

"Only because you're so inspiring." She rubbed her hands against his chest, pleased when she felt his heart pick up speed. "You're also sexy as all get out. When I found you half-naked in your office, I had the naughtiest thoughts."

"Shame on you," he murmured as he stroked her back. She trembled with pleasure when he slid one hand over the curve of her hip and cupped her buttock, nestling her even closer to him. "But I guess I shouldn't scold you, because I'm having some naughty thoughts myself, right now."

"I'll tell you mine if you'll tell me yours," she challenged with a flirtatious bat of her lashes.

"Let's save them for some day when we're alone," he whispered as he lowered his lips to hers.

Christy decided that heaven couldn't be as wonderful as the feel of Adam's lips, and she wound her arms around his neck, buried her fingers in his hair, and kissed him back ardently.

Adam groaned softly when she teased at his lips with her tongue, and though he kept telling himself that they were in a public place, he couldn't refrain from letting her inside. Her tongue danced playfully in his mouth, and he groaned again and pulled her hips firmly against his.

"Don't stop!" Christy exclaimed breathlessly when he jerked his head away from the kiss.

"Christy, we're behind a potted plant in the corridor. Someone could see us at any moment," he reminded between ragged breaths. She fit against him so perfectly that he'd have sworn she'd been made for him.

She dropped her forehead to his chest. "I know some-one could see us, but I can't help myself. Every time you touch me, I get all hot and quivery inside. Do you think it's possible that I'm a latent sex maniac?"

Adam laughed lightly and kneaded her shoulders. "Well, if you are, then join the club, because I get all hot and quivery inside when you touch me."

He caught her chin, raising her head so that he could look into her eyes. His expression was solemn when he said, "Things are moving too fast between us, Christy, and I think we need to work hard at slowing it down. If we make love, it should be because our heads say it's what we want, not because of our hormones."

She gave him a rueful smile. "I agree, so I think I'd better make a mad dash for the car. A brisk run in be-low-freezing temperatures is exactly what I need to cool off. I'll see you in the morning."

She slipped out of his arms and was gone before Adam could lever himself away from the wall, and he hurried to the doors, scowling as he watched her race across the icy parking lot.

"Dammit, slow down before you fall and break your beautiful little neck," he muttered.

She made it to her car without mishap. Adam shook his head as he watched her car disappear. She was a delight, but he had a sinking feeling that she was also going to be one hell of a handful of trouble.

CHRISTY'S HOUSE WAS two doors down from her par-ents', and when she climbed out of her car, she auto-matically glanced in their direction. The moment she did, she realized that she had a serious problem brewing over her decision to date Adam. Only her mother could advise her on how to handle it. She skirted her neighbor's backyard and entered her parents' kitchen door.

"Christy, are you just getting home from work?" Ilona asked as she glanced up in surprise from loading dishes into the dishwasher.

"Nope. I'm just getting home from a dinner date," Christy answered as she searched her mother's face for any sign of distress. Her mother had arthritis, which tended to act up during cold weather, and Christy knew that she'd walk on hot coals before she'd admit that she was in pain. To Christy's relief, there was no sign of discomfort.

"You went to dinner dressed as an elf?" Ilona exclaimed in disbelief.

"He was dressed in red jogging clothes, so we were color coordinated," Christy replied as she walked across the room, kissed her mother's cheek and then helped herself to a sugar cookie from the cookie jar. "Where's Pop?"

"Resting his eyes in front of the television," Ilona grumbled.

Christy laughed. For as long as she could remember, her parents had squabbled over her father's habit of falling asleep in front of the television and then insisting that he hadn't been napping, just resting his eyes.

"Well, I'm glad to see things are back to normal." She settled at the old oak table. As she nibbled on the cookie, she said, "I'm also glad Pop's asleep, because I have a feeling that come morning, he isn't going to be very happy with me, and I need your help in dealing with him."

"What's wrong? Trouble at work?" Ilona said in concern as she sat down at the table.

"Not the kind of trouble you're referring to," Christy reassured. "I've met a man, and Pop isn't going to like it."

"So, what else is new? You know as well as I do that you could bring home the Pope and your father would find fault with him." Ilona narrowed her eyes. "You've never cared what your father thought about the men you've dated before. Why are you worried about it now?"

"Because I've never felt this way about a man before," Christy admitted with a heartfelt sigh. "The trouble is, Pop has already warned me off the guy, and when he finds out I'm ignoring him, he's going to hit the ceiling."

"Who's the man?"

"My boss at the mall."

"Scrooge?" Ilona responded in astonishment, and Christy groaned. When her father had first christened Adam with the nickname, she hadn't seen any harm in it, but now it could definitely prove to be a problem. She loved her parents to distraction, but they both tended to speak before thinking. What would she do if they called Adam "Scrooge" to his face?

"His name's Adam, Mom. Adam Worth, and he isn't a Scrooge. He's a very nice man."

"And your father doesn't like him."

"I don't think he dislikes him," Christy hedged, "but he thinks Adam's a workaholic."

"And?" Ilona prompted, accurately sensing there was more.

"And he's thirty-seven years old," Christy stated in a rush.

"I see." Ilona folded her hands on the table. "You're right. When your father hears that you're dating him, his blood pressure is going to skyrocket."

Christy paled, because she hadn't thought of that. She'd never forgive herself if she upset her father so badly she made him ill. But what was she supposed to do? Refuse to date Adam after practically twisting his arm to get him to see her?

"Good heavens, Christy, don't look so panic-stricken. Your father will get over it. He always does."

"I know, but the doctor told him to avoid stress, and if I upset him, he could—"

"Stop it," Ilona chided as she reached out and took Christy's hand. "Honey, you can't live your life based on whether or not it might upset your father. Even if you wanted to, I wouldn't let you. Do you have any idea how powerful a weapon we'd be placing in his hands if he realized that all he had to do was clutch his chest to get his way? Why, he'd become a full-fledged tyrant instead of a grumpy despot!"

"That's true," Christy agreed with a wan smile. "But—"

"There are no buts about this, Christy," Ilona declared. "If your father doesn't like you dating Adam Worth, that's tough. Besides, he shouldn't be haranguing you about any man after his own experiences with my father. Have I never told you that Dad hated Robert when we first got married?"

"You're joking!" Christy exclaimed, propping her elbows on the table and cradling her chin in her hands, fascinated by her mother's disclosure. "I wasn't very old when Gramps died, but from what I remember, he and Pop were great pals."

"Oh, they were, but it was several years after we were married before Dad decided that Robert wasn't such a bad sort. So, you just have a good time with your new

gentleman friend and let me worry about your father. I
know how to handle him."

"Thanks." Christy kissed her mother. Then she said,
"Adam's age doesn't bother *you*, does it?"

Ilona shrugged. "I'll admit that I'd like to see you dating someone closer to your own age. But as long as you're
happy, then I'm happy."

"Christy?" her father mumbled in confusion as he
came into the kitchen, his hair mussed and his eyes still
drooping from sleep. "What are you doing here at this
time of night? And why are you still in costume?"

"I had a dinner date, Pop, and I decided to stop by and
say hello to Mom." She hopped up and gave him a
smacking kiss on the cheek. "Sorry, but I've gotta run. I
have a ton of film to develop. See you in the morning."

"Who in their right mind would take you to dinner
dressed as an elf?" Robert called after her as she hurried
out the door.

Christy knew she was being a coward, but she pre-
tended she didn't hear him. She did, however, suc-
cinctly hear her mother say, "Sit down, Robert. We need
to have a little chat."

5

ADAM WASN'T SURE what he'd expected Christy's home to look like, but certainly not the old Victorian house he saw when he pulled into her drive. Yet, as he surveyed the gingerbread trim and the wide front porch, he couldn't picture her in any other style of environment. He climbed out of his four-wheel drive and walked to her front door, beside which hung an unobtrusive wrought-iron sign that read: Portrait Studio. For the past two days, he'd fought the urge to cancel their date. He was going to go through with it. It was time that he stopped playing it safe and took a few chances in life.

The door flew open, and Christy greeted him with a breathless "Hello." At the sight of her, he forgot his reservations about being here. Innumerable times he'd imagined what she'd look like with her hair down, but he could never have conjured up the vision before him now of her beautiful golden tresses, flowing halfway down her back.

He might have stared at her for hours in mesmerized fascination if there hadn't been a sudden fluttering of colorful wings that came to rest on her shoulder, followed by an earsplitting wolf whistle and a squawking announcement: "Sexy man alert. Sexy man alert."

"Who is that?" Adam asked with a laugh as he found himself peering into the black beady eyes of a huge red-and-green parrot.

Christy grinned and gestured for him to enter. "This is Gypsy. As you can tell, she has great taste in men."

"Somehow I didn't expect you to have a parrot as a pet," he remarked. "You look more like the cuddly-kitten type."

She closed the door behind him. "I have a couple of those, too, though they tend to make themselves scarce when Gypsy's on the loose. I'm afraid she's a bit of a bully."

"Your cats are afraid of a bird? I would have thought it would be the other way around," he commented as his eyes glided in appreciation from the top of her head to the tips of her toes. She was wearing an oversize, shocking-pink sweatshirt that hung to her knees, lemon-yellow tights and fuzzy fluorescent-purple slippers. On anyone else, the outfit and color combination would have looked bizarre, but she managed to carry it off with panache. She also looked so sexy that he had to stuff his hands into his pockets to keep from snatching her into his arms.

"Gypsy doesn't know she's a bird," Christy explained while doing a survey of her own. Adam was handsome in a suit—and devastating in the dungarees and sweatshirt he was wearing today—but she still preferred him au naturel. Or at least, she preferred the top portion of him that way. She'd have to reserve judgment on the bottom half until she'd seen it with her own eyes. Hopefully the opportunity would present itself soon.

"What does she think she is?" Adam asked, trying to control his libido beneath Christy's bold gaze. He'd never had a woman look at him so brazenly, and his stomach knotted as her eyes paused for an overly long moment in the area of his belt buckle.

"Your guess is as good as mine," she answered. "Are you early or am I running late? As you can tell, I'm not dressed. I've been locked in the darkroom for hours."

Adam glanced at his watch. "I'm seven minutes early. Want me to leave and come back?"

"No," Christy murmured as she shooed Gypsy off her shoulder and stepped closer to him. "It's fashionable for a lady to be late, so let's use those seven extra minutes to be totally indecent."

"What's your definition of indecent?" he asked as he wrapped his arms around her.

"Give me an example of your definition, and I'll tell you if it matches mine," she suggested throatily.

Adam's libido went on a rampage at her words. Did she know what she was doing to him? He tangled his fingers in her hair and levered her head back until he had a full view of her face.

"Make sure you know what you want before you start playing games with me," he told her gruffly. "Because I'm afraid you might not like my rules."

"That works both ways, Adam," she whispered, quivering at the passion glowing in his eyes. Why was he standing there lecturing her when he should be kissing her? "The difference between us is that I make up the rules as I go along, so you'd better be prepared to stay one step ahead of me."

"Damn, you're the most frustrating woman I've ever met," he muttered as he lowered his lips to hers.

But Christy wasn't insulted. His husky tone had assured her that his words were as much an endearment as they were a curse.

She wound her arms around his neck and arched against him, sighing in pleasure when he caught her hips and pulled her hard against him. His erection made her stomach contract in aching pleasure.

This is what it's supposed to be like. This is what I've been searching for, longing for, even praying for.

"We've got to stop," Adam gasped as he buried his face in her hair. "We're supposed to be moving slowly. We have to be certain this is right."

Christy's laugh was hollow as she rested her ear against his chest and listened to the galloping beat of his heart. "If this isn't right, Adam, then I'm all in favor of wrong."

"If I thought you had the experience to back up those words, I'd take you up on them," he said as he released her and stepped back.

He'd placed no more than a few inches between them, but it felt like a chasm. "And what makes you think I'm not experienced?" she asked, wanting to close that distance, but sensing that it would be the wrong move.

Adam reached into his pocket and pulled out a small, gaily wrapped package. "Because an experienced woman wouldn't get as excited about this gift as I know you will."

"You brought me a present?" she exclaimed in delight as she accepted the package. "What is it?"

"Open it and find out."

"But part of the fun is guessing. Is it all right to squeeze it? Can I shake it?"

Adam could only shake his head, because she looked like a charming child, yet he knew she was all woman. His body was still aching from the kiss they'd just shared.

"Is that a yes or a no?" she asked.

"You can shake it, but I wouldn't squeeze it."

She brought the package up to her ear and gave it a gentle shake, and Adam was captivated by her ingenuous expression. He'd bought the gift on impulse, because when he'd seen it this morning, it had reminded him of her. It wasn't expensive, but he'd known that she'd be enamored with it.

"Shaking it doesn't tell me anything," she said with a disgruntled sigh. "It doesn't even rattle."

His lips twitched. "So, open it and find out what it is."

She grabbed his hand and led him to a nearby over-stuffed sofa. When they were seated, she carefully untied the ribbon and then just as carefully undid the wrapping.

"I would have guessed that you were a rip-'em-open kind of girl," he remarked as she folded the paper and placed it on the sofa beside her.

"Good heavens, no! The best part of a present is the anticipation. You have to delay opening it as long as possible. Oh, Adam!" she exclaimed a moment later as she lifted the lid off the box and pushed aside the tissue paper to reveal a soft-sculpture angel designed as a tree ornament.

Adam had to swallow against the sudden lump in his throat when she threw her arms around his neck, hugging him exuberantly as she cried, "Thank you. She's the most adorable thing I've ever seen!"

"I thought she was rather cute myself, and you're welcome," he said roughly. Why was he suddenly feeling so choked up? He had expected this reaction from her, and perhaps that was exactly why he was so touched. It was the first time he'd ever purchased a gift that he knew would be accepted with such genuine enthusiasm.

"Come on," she urged as she grabbed his hand and pulled him up beside her. Then she took him to the back of the house. "We have to hang her on the tree."

Adam had been so wrapped up in her that he hadn't realized they'd been in the waiting room of her portrait studio until she led him down a hallway past a door that was filled with props and camera equipment, and past another that was closed and had Darkroom printed across it in bold black letters. She threw open a third door and he came to a halt, his jaw dropping.

Evergreen Mall was a holiday showcase, but Christy's living room took that term into another dimension. There wasn't an inch of space in the room that didn't reflect the holiday season. Even her furniture wore slipcovers of red-and-green velvet with Santa Clauses, snowmen, elves and Christmas trees appliquéd on them. But the eye-catcher was a Christmas tree so huge that it nearly filled one wall, and rose to the top of her twelve-foot ceiling. As far as he could see, not one branch was barren, nor was any decoration the same.

"Where in the world are you going to put her?" he asked as he studied the tree incredulously.

"I'm not going to put her anywhere. You are."

He peered down at her askance. "Me?"

"You gave her to me, so you should pick the best spot to display her."

He glanced from her to the tree and back to her, certain she was joking. But the look on her face told him she was completely serious. "I don't know, Christy. I'm, uh, not very good at hanging ornaments."

"Don't be silly," she chided as she handed him the angel. "You just go over to the tree and put her where you think she belongs. Isn't that what you did when you were a kid?"

"Yeah," Adam lied as he cautiously approached the tree. The truth was, his mother's version of a Christmas tree had been a silver-foil concoction that she'd never let him touch, and the tree at his father's home had always been decorated when he wasn't around.

"What about here?" he asked when he found an empty branch a few inches above his head.

"Perfect," Christy said. "Now that that problem is taken care of, I'm going to put Gypsy into her cage and run upstairs and change. Make yourself at home. There's a fresh pot of coffee in the kitchen, and if that doesn't appeal to you, there's a kettle on the stove and a tin of herbal tea next to it. The kitchen is that way," she finished, pointing toward a short hallway.

She disappeared up the stairs before Adam could reply, and he wandered toward the kitchen. He didn't want anything to drink, but he was curious about her house.

The kitchen was large, clean, and cluttered with every imaginable cooking device. He'd never thought of Christy as a cook, but as he examined the room, he could envision her at the stove. She probably was a gourmet chef, and the more obscure the dish, the better.

The kitchen opened into a small dining room, which contained a round antique table with clawed feet and a matching hutch. It led into another room that he supposed would have been a sitting room at the turn of the century. It was decorated with antique bric-a-brac, a comfortable-looking sofa, and a portable television set. It invited a person to sit down, kick off their shoes and prop their feet on the coffee table.

He wandered back into the kitchen, speculating that his own sterile apartment would be about as inviting to Christy as an operating room. That thought disturbed him. The differences between them were so numerous that he had to wonder what was drawing them to each other. Or to be exact, what was drawing Christy to him? With another woman, he would have said it was a simple matter of physical attraction. Christy's feelings for him were clearly more complex than that.

.

"You don't like Revere Ware pots?" Christy asked from the doorway.

"What?" Adam murmured.

He hadn't heard her enter the room, and his gaze flicked over her. She'd pulled on a pair of denims and a green sweatshirt, tucked her hair beneath a bright red ski cap with green Christmas trees embroidered on it, pulled on a matching red parka, and held red-and-green-striped mittens in her hand. How could a woman look so cute and sexy at the same time?

"You were scowling at the copper skillet on the wall," she said teasingly. "I assumed that you don't like Revere Ware."

"I didn't even notice the skillet. I was thinking."

Christy squelched the impulse to ask what he'd been thinking about. His expression was so solemn she suspected he regretted coming today.

Darn! She should have kept a better watch on the clock and been ready to leave the moment he arrived so he wouldn't have had time to think. Admittedly, she was as reluctant as Adam, avoiding getting ready as a means of self-protection. During the past few days he'd been distant with her—not exactly withdrawn and certainly not rude, but definitely reticent. Since she half believed he would cancel their date at the last minute, she'd rationalized she wouldn't be so disappointed if she wasn't dressed and waiting.

"Well, you're not supposed to be thinking this afternoon. From this moment on, you are to do nothing but react to your surroundings. Enjoy them. Soak them in. Relax. Got that?"

"Got it. Let's go," he said. If they didn't get out of there, they weren't going to spend the next few hours sledding, and Adam wasn't ready to make love with her.

He needed more time to get to know Christy—and especially to figure out why, of all the available men in Colorado Springs, he was the one she'd chosen to be with.

"WHERE ARE WE GOING?" Adam questioned after they'd loaded the sled into the back of his car.

"My parents own some mountain property twenty miles on the other side of Woodland Park. It has the best slope for sledding I've ever seen," she said.

Adam nodded and headed toward the highway. They were quiet, but it was a comfortable silence that he found soothing and a refreshing change from his hectic office. But after they'd maneuvered their way through the congested traffic and hit the open highway on the other side of town, he'd had enough of silence.

"I like your house," he remarked. "Do you own it?"

Christy adjusted her seat belt so she could face him. "The bank lets me pretend that I do. They promised that as long as I keep up my mortgage payments for the next thirty years, they'll continue to let me carry out the fantasy. What about you? Do you own a house?"

Adam shook his head. "I've never had time for a house, but I've always dreamed of owning one. Maybe someday I can make it come true."

There was something so wistful in his expression, and it tugged at Christy's heartstrings. She could sense his loneliness.

"How come you've never been married?" she asked.

"What makes you think I've never been married?" he countered.

Christy grimaced, realizing she'd stuck her foot in her mouth. He wouldn't be pleased if he learned his secretary had been discussing his personal life with Bertha's daughter.

"I don't know. I guess you just look like a man who's never been married," she improvised. "Have you?"

"No. I was engaged once, but it didn't work out. How about you? Have you ever been married?"

"No. Like you, I was engaged once, but it didn't work out."

Adam found her answer surprising. He couldn't imagine any man foolish enough to walk away from her. "I know it's none of my business, but do you mind if I ask what happened?"

"I don't mind. It was a college romance. When we graduated, I wanted to start saving for a down payment on a house and a minivan. He wanted to start saving for a downpayment on a condominium and a sports car. It suddenly dawned on me that our perceptions of marriage weren't quite the same."

"That must have been rough," Adam said as he glanced surreptitiously at her. If she was upset by the memory, she didn't show it.

She shrugged. "It was rough, but not catastrophic. I guess that's when I figured out that I was in love with love and not in love with him. So, what happened to your engagement?"

This time, Adam shrugged. "I guess our ideas of marriage weren't quite the same, either. I wanted to save enough money to open my own mall and ensure us a secure future. She wanted to see the world and worry about the future when all our money ran out. When I refused to quit my job and become a vagabond, she quit me."

"That must have hurt," Christy murmured. Did he see the correlation between their stories? They'd both been looking for security, while the people they'd been in love with had been looking for excitement.

"It did hurt," Adam confessed. "But I'm over it and have been for a long time." He smiled. "Have I ever told you how beautiful you are?"

"No," Christy whispered. Desire hit her with such intensity that if her seat belt hadn't been restraining her, she would have thrown herself into his arms.

"Well, remind me to tell you sometime," Adam rasped, gripping the steering wheel until his knuckles were white. It was the only way he could keep from slamming on the brakes and pulling her into his arms.

Once again they were silent, but this time it wasn't soothing. The sexual tension in the car was so thick, Adam was surprised it didn't fog the windows. They reached their turnoff a short time later, however, and he welcomed the bumpy drive along a snow-covered, rutted mountain road that required all his concentration.

Christy was just as grateful that they were nearing their destination, because she needed some space—and badly. She wasn't a novice to physical attraction, but she'd never had a man affect her so deeply or make her feel so out of control.

It had to be love. Only love could feel this heady and yet so frightening at the same time. And she was frightened, because it was happening so fast and she had no way of knowing if Adam felt the same way about her. It was evident that he desired her. It was also evident that he liked her. But desire and like didn't always add up to love.

"The slope is on the other side of that stand of trees," she told him, pointing toward a cluster of pines ahead of them.

"Right," Adam said.

When he braked to a stop a few minutes later, Christy leaped out of the car, yelling over her shoulder, "Wait until you see this view. It's breathtaking!"

Adam watched her run to the top of the slope. The snow rose ankle-deep on her knee-high boots, and his gaze wandered up her shapely legs until they came to rest on her rounded posterior. She was right: The view was breathtaking. It was also arousing as hell.

With a muttered curse, he climbed out and put on his parka before he went to join her.

"Well, what do you think?" she asked when he reached her side.

"I'd forgotten how beautiful the mountains are at this time of year," Adam murmured in awe as he took in the valley below them. The highway wasn't far away, but it was blocked from sight by the towering skeletons of aspens and the full-bodied boughs of evergreens. The snow was pristine and glistened like a carpet of diamonds beneath the afternoon sun. Snow-covered mountain peaks loomed around them, and Pikes Peak stood in front of them, its summit shrouded in low-hanging clouds.

"They're also fun," Christy said as she grabbed his arm and started dragging him back toward the car. "Let's get the sled."

"What's the rush?" he demanded with an indulgent chuckle.

"Don't you feel that hill calling to you?" she asked excitedly.

"Nope."

"You're hopeless," she muttered as they reached the car.

Adam grinned as he retrieved the sled and set it on the ground. "Now what?"

"Now the fun begins. Where's your hat?"

"I didn't bring one."

"That's what I was afraid of." She strode to the front of the car, opened the passenger door and pulled a psychedelic-colored ski cap from her purse.

Adam eyed the cap dubiously when she handed it to him. "You don't really expect me to wear that eyesore."

"Of course I do." She gave a mock affronted sniff. "If you don't, your ears are going to freeze and fall off. I can see the headlines now—Prominent Mall Owner Loses Ears While Sledding."

He laughed, then grabbed the hat and tugged it on. "How's that?"

She perched her mittened hands on her hips and eyed him appraisingly. "Very rakish. Where are your gloves? You did bring gloves, didn't you?"

"Of course." He retrieved his gloves from his pocket and pulled them on. Grabbing the lead on the sled, he followed her to the crest of the hill.

"How long has it been since you've been on a sled?" she asked.

Adam shrugged. "Twenty years or so."

"That means I get to steer."

"Oh, yeah? Why?"

"Because I'd never trust my neck to a rusty sledder. That hill looks gentle, but believe me, by the time you reach the bottom, you feel as if you've entered the Indianapolis 500." She climbed onto the sled, scooted forward and ordered, "Climb on."

Adam stared at her, realizing that this innocent little sledding trip was going to bring them into a proximity that was far more intimate than that of any kiss they'd shared. Suddenly he wished he was back in his office with his piles of paperwork sitting in front of him. At the mall he could acknowledge his attraction to her, indulge himself in a few brief kisses, and still remain safe. Once he climbed onto the back of her sled, he'd be stepping into her world, and there would be no turning back.

It was on the tip of his tongue to tell her he wanted to go home, but she tilted her head and looked up at him, her eyes sparkling with anticipation and her lips curved into an excited smile. He couldn't any more have denied her her sleigh ride than he could have stopped breathing.

He chastised himself for being a fool as he climbed onto the back of the sled, wrapped his arms around her waist and pushed them off. Desire shot through him as their descent pressed her buttocks deep into the cradle of his thighs. But his libido was the last thing on his mind when they flew over a hump and Christy lost control. Before Adam knew what was happening, they were both sprawled in the snow. He came up sputtering, only to find Christy lying beside him and rolling with laughter.

"I think I should have asked how long it's been since you've been on a sled," he grumbled good-naturedly.

"Just last year, but the first run is always precarious."

She sat up, brushing the snow from her jacket before pulling her cap off her head and shaking it out. Her hair tumbled down her back in a disheveled halo, and a new surge of desire swept through Adam. His breathing became shallow, and his blood heated, but Christy seemed unaware of his response as she tucked her hair back under her cap, leaped to her feet and ran to retrieve the sled.

Adam brushed off the snow and rose to follow her. This was going to be a painfully long afternoon. He just hoped that the brisk winter air would have the same effect as a cold shower.

They managed several successful rides down the hill before they had another crash. This time it was Adam who was laughing uproariously as he literally dug Christy out of a gigantic snowdrift.

"You think that's funny, do you?" she grumbled in mock indignation when he hauled her to her feet. "Let's see what you think about this!"

Before Adam knew what was happening, she'd thrown a snowball at him and taken off running. Adam grabbed a handful of snow and threw it at her just as she raced behind a tree. For the next several minutes they fired snowball after snowball as they ducked behind trees and rocks. Christy's aim was better than his, and he was soon covered with snow from head to foot.

Finally he yelled "Uncle!" as he laughingly sat down in the snow, trying to recall the last time he'd had so much fun.

Christy swaggered toward him, a smug grin of victory on her face. "You, Adam Worth, have nonexistent reflexes."

"Oh, yeah?" He leaned forward, grabbed her ankle and tumbled her into his arms, drawling, "Now, what was that you were saying about nonexistent reflexes?"

"You cheated!" she accused breathlessly as she rested her head on his shoulder and looked up at him. "You surrendered, and then you attacked."

"You should always approach your prisoners with caution," he told her. "A man will leap at the opportunity to turn the tables on his victor."

"So, now that I'm your prisoner, what are you going to do with me?" she inquired with a bat of her lashes and a come-hither smile.

The heat that engulfed Adam should have melted the snow within a fifty-foot radius. "I guess I'll have to persuade you to tell me all your secrets."

"Torture is prohibited under the Geneva Convention," she murmured as she wrapped her arms around his neck.

"Yeah, but all is fair in love and war," he mumbled as he lowered his lips to hers.

Christy shivered beneath his kiss, but it wasn't from the brisk air blowing through the valley or the snow melting through her clothes. It was from the tenderness and gentleness of Adam's kiss. It made her feel precious and cherished. It also made her ache with need. When she felt him withdrawing from the kiss, she held on tightly, refusing to let him go.

But eventually Adam managed to disengage himself from her embrace, and he smiled wryly as he said, "Honey, this is not the best place to get carried away. We could end up with some very embarrassing frostbitten parts."

"It would be worth it," she said. Adam had never looked more handsome than he did at this moment. His cheeks were ruddy from the cold, his eyes were dark pools of desire, and his expression was free of tension— or at least the lines of tension brought on by overwork. "I want to make love with you, Adam."

She was both hurt and disappointed when Adam shook his head. "I'm not ready to take that big a step, Christy."

"Don't you want me?"

He closed his eyes and groaned. "Dammit, you're sitting in my lap, so you know full well that I want you."

"Then what's the problem?"

"I need more time," he said as he opened his eyes and frowned at her. "I'm not like you. I can't rush in where angels fear to tread. I have to dissect and analyze. I have to weigh the pros against the cons. I have to know what to expect before I make love with you."

"Good heavens, it sounds as if you make love the same way you eat croissants—systematically," Christy complained as she slipped off his lap and sat down in front of him.

"Don't be ridiculous," Adam replied with a scowl.

"I'm not being ridiculous," she defended as she hugged her knees to her chest. "You're talking about dissecting and analyzing, and I'm talking about spontaneity. The worst part is, you want to do all your dissecting and analyzing so you'll know what to expect, when the answer to that is as clear as the nose on your face."

"And what is this answer that's so clear?" he asked impatiently.

She smiled. "Pleasure, Adam. Pure, unadulterated pleasure."

"It's more complicated than that, and you know it," he said with a snort of derision. "What happens to us when we crawl out of bed? You're a pie-in-the-sky optimist and I'm a dyed-in-the-wool pessimist. You bounce through life like it's a romp in the snow, and I plod through life looking for quicksand. There are too many differences between us, and a few forays between the sheets aren't going to make them go away."

"You're right there," she stated so cheerfully that Adam wanted to growl at her. "But it's those differences that are in our favor."

"Dream on," Adam retorted with a plaintive roll of his eyes. "Differences cause problems."

"Not if you use them to your advantage," she countered. "You say I'm a bouncy optimist and you're a plodding pessimist. It sounds to me as if you will ground me when I need to be grounded, and I'll lift you up when you need to be lifted up. When you look at it from that viewpoint, we're the perfect match."

Adam gave an adamant shake of his head. "It sounds wonderful in theory, Christy, but like most theories, it's guaranteed to blow up in our faces."

"No," she murmured as she shifted to her knees, placed her hands on his shoulders and leaned toward him until their noses almost brushed. "*This* will keep it from blowing up in our faces."

Adam knew she was going to kiss him. He also knew that he should stop her, but his heart overrode his common sense when her lips touched his. He groaned as he fell backward, pulling her over him. He wanted—needed—what she was offering, because he was tired of trudging through life alone. Would it be so wrong to let her help lessen the load for a while? Would it be so wrong to indulge himself in a few of life's pleasures for once?

Yes, his conscience answered, *because you know damn good and well that it can't work. And when it doesn't, what are you going to have?*

Memories, he answered as Christy tangled her legs with his and her tongue invaded his mouth. *Beautiful, passionate memories.*

Before his conscience could offer him any further objections, he rolled her off him, jumped to his feet and grabbed her hand, pulling her up beside him. "If we intend to get in a few more sled rides before the sun goes down, we'd better get moving."

Christy didn't know whether to continue arguing with him or kick him in the shins, so she fell into step beside him instead. As she marched up the hill, she resolved that she wasn't going to let him dissect and analyze what was happening between them, or weigh the pros and cons of their relationship. She was a woman—not a business proposition. And she made herself a vow that by the time the day was over, Adam was going to understand that.

6

ADAM STOOD WITH CHRISTY at the top of the hill, watching the sun sink on the horizon. The sky was an indescribable vermilion that made him wish he had the ability to capture its beauty on canvas.

"I think I missed the sunsets the most when I lived back east," Christy told him. "Isn't it absolutely glorious?"

Adam looped his arm around her shoulder. "It is glorious, and I haven't watched a sunset in years. Thank you for a wonderful afternoon."

"Did you really enjoy it?" she asked, smiling up at him.

"Every minute," he replied. "But the next time, I insist on steering the sled a few times."

Christy's heart skipped a beat at his words. If he was alluding to a next time, then maybe a relationship between them wasn't impossible.

She grinned at him impishly. "As long as they're solo flights, you can steer the sled all you want."

He laughed and pulled her into his arms for a hug. "You are impossible, incorrigible, and positively irreverent."

"I know," she said, snuggling her cold nose into his coat. "It comes from being a doted-upon only child. So if you have any complaints, you'll have to take them up with my parents."

"I'd be afraid Robert would skin me alive if I even hinted that you weren't perfect."

"Adam, you're talking about Santa Claus!" she scolded in feigned dismay.

"I know," he replied, gazing down into her upturned face. Her cheeks and the tip of her nose were bright red, but she was saved from looking twelve years old by the warm intelligence glowing in her eyes, and by her softly parted, very feminine lips.

He placed his mouth over hers in a gentle, searching kiss, promising himself that he'd take just a taste and then release her. But when her lips parted eagerly beneath his, he groaned and swept her tightly against him, giving free rein to the hunger he'd been battling all day.

Christy lost her breath as he clasped her to his chest totally unprepared for the powerful surge of desire that swept through her. Her pulse was pounding, her heart was racing, and her body temperature was rising in direct proportion to the increased heaviness in her lower abdomen.

She wrapped her arms around his neck as he slid a hand beneath her buttocks and pulled her intimately against him, giving her proof that she was affecting him as intensely as he was her. When he released her from the kiss, she once again buried her face against his coat, unable to decide which of them was breathing the most raggedly.

"We'd better get going," Adam eventually said, his voice a husky rasp.

"I suppose so," Christy acknowledged, though she didn't make any effort to move from his embrace.

"How about if we stop for dinner on the way home?" he asked.

Christy leaned her head back and regarded him in bemusement. "What about the mall?"

"What about it?"

"You've been away from it for a good five or six hours. Aren't you worried that it's crumbled to the ground without you there to shore it up?"

He shrugged in unconcern. "If it has, there isn't much I can do about it now. So, how about dinner?"

"Mexican?" she suggested before he could change his mind.

"You've got it."

A short time later, Adam helped Christy out of the car and escorted her into a small Mexican restaurant whose sign boasted that it was a family-operated business. They were met by a solemn young boy of about ten who informed them he was the maître d', then bowed formally and led them to a table.

"He's adorable, isn't he?" Adam murmured when the boy had walked away.

"Yes, he is," Christy agreed. "You really like kids, don't you?"

"What's not to like?"

"That's true, but a lot of men are uncomfortable around children. The few I've met who are comfortable around them usually come from large families. Is your family large?"

"No. I have a half sister. Her name's Danielle, but we call her Dani." He smiled. "She's expecting her first child in February, and she'll make a great mother. She's such a Pollyanna."

It was a strange description to apply to one's sister, but before Christy could pursue it, an attractive young waitress approached the table and asked if they'd like a drink before dinner. Christy decided on a margarita, but Adam opted for club soda with a twist of lime, telling her that since he was driving and the roads were icy in spots, he wanted to keep a clear head.

While they waited for their drinks, they scanned the menu. By the time the waitress returned they were ready to order. Once the waitress was gone again, Adam asked, "Up on the mountain, you said you'd lived back east. When was that?"

"When I graduated from college, I was offered an apprenticeship with a group of free-lance photographers in Philadelphia and I jumped at the chance," Christy answered. "I'd just broken up with Curt and felt that a change of scenery was in order. Besides, I needed to do a lot of growing up, and I knew I'd never do that if I lived around Mom and Pop. If you think Pop is overprotective now, you should have seen him three years ago. The way he hovered over me, you would have thought I was still in diapers."

"Don't you think you're being a bit rough on him?" Adam inquired at her sardonic tone. "I'm sure he was worried about you. After all, you'd just broken up with your fiancé, and an experience like that can be painful."

"I know his reasons were altruistic, Adam, but that type of devotion breeds dependence, and I was already too dependent on my parents. I had to learn to take responsibility for myself because my parents' ages alone guarantee that they won't always be around to help me through the rough times. That point was really nailed home when Pop had his heart attack."

The moment the words were out of Christy's mouth, she wanted to snatch them back. Adam's spine straightened and his frown told her he wasn't pleased by the revelation."

"When did your father have a heart attack?" he asked stiffly.

"Six months ago," Christy replied.

"Dammit, Christy, why didn't you tell me that?" he demanded in a low, furious whisper. "If I'd know he'd had a heart attack, I would never have—"

"Hired us," she finished for him. She propped her forearms on the table and leaned toward him. "And that's exactly why I didn't offer the information. After the heart attack, Pop was having terrible spells of depression because he felt old and useless. The doctor thought that playing Santa Claus would be good therapy for him, and it has been. His spirits have improved a hundred percent."

When Adam continued to scowl at her, she added, "If you'd asked about his health, I would have told you. But you didn't ask, so I didn't offer. Maybe that was wrong, but I had cleared it with his doctor, and I assure you that I would never have applied for the job if I'd felt there was a possibility we couldn't fulfill our contract. If you feel that I owe you an apology, then I'm sorry. But if I had to do it again, I would."

Even though Adam knew he should be furious with her, he felt his temper waning as she looked at him contritely. It was true that he probably wouldn't have hired the Knights, had he known about Robert's recent heart attack—doctor's approval or not. He also knew that if he put himself in her place, he'd probably have done the same thing. Still, it grated that she hadn't been honest with him; total honesty was the one thing he had come to expect from her.

Not that she had been dishonest, he assured himself. As she'd said, he hadn't asked, and maybe that was where the rub came in. Normally he would have asked about both of their medical histories. But Christy and her father had taken him by storm. He had hired them without making any of the normal inquiries that an employer was obligated to make. If he was going to be angry with anyone, he supposed he should be angry with himself.

"Are you going to forgive me?" Christy asked when his silence stretched to the point that she was ready to shred her napkin.

"I shouldn't," he said with a wry twist of his lips. "But, yes, I forgive you. In future, however, I would suggest that you don't withhold that sort of information. Another employer might not be as understanding as I am."

Fortunately, their meal arrived at that moment. To lighten the conversation, Christy began asking him questions about the different places he'd lived during his career as a mall manager. Soon their conversation became more personal, and as they talked they discovered that they had more in common than they'd thought. Both were fascinated with Colorado history, loved to explore old ghost towns and had a passion for museums.

As they lingered over coffee, Adam told her about his dreams for the mall and Christy shared her aspirations for her portrait studio. By the time Adam helped her into his car, Christy had come to the conclusion that he was everything she wanted in a man. The question was, Was she what he wanted in a woman? Even if she was, would he still analyze out of existence any possibility of a future for them?

Under the cover of darkness, she studied him, mulling over all she'd learned about him. Her mind kept returning to the day he'd been so upset when he'd had his picture taken with Santa. Initially she'd assumed that he'd merely been angry at her and her father for teasing him. But now she recognized it was more than that. He'd been hurt—really hurt—but why? Until she understood that, her relationship with Adam would remain precarious at best.

Sensing her scrutiny, Adam turned his head toward her when he braked at a stoplight. "Is something wrong?"

"No," Christy answered as her gaze roamed over his face. His hair had tumbled across his forehead. The shadow of an evening beard highlighted a tiny scar on his chin. She wanted to touch the scar and ask him how he had gotten it. She wanted to test the texture of his whiskers with her palm. She wanted to smooth the lock of hair away from his brow. She wanted to perform all the tender gestures that a lover would perform. Unfortunately, she wasn't his lover. "I was just looking at you. It's a very pleasant pastime."

Her words hit Adam with a sensual force. He'd never had a woman say anything like that to him. He'd been told he was handsome, of course, and a few women had even told him he was sexy, but those were standard lines. There was nothing standard about Christy's words.

When the light changed, he stepped on the accelerator and avoided responding to Christy's remark. He wanted her, and she wanted him. But did he have the courage to take the plunge?

"WOULD YOU LIKE TO COME in for some hot chocolate?" Christy asked when Adam pulled into her drive. Incurable optimist that she was, she made the offer expecting him to decline.

Not only did Adam need to get back to the mall, but he needed to get away from Christy. Things were happening too fast between them. She'd only started working at the mall four days ago, so they'd known each other less than a week. Well—more like three weeks if he started counting from the day she first came into his office; but even three weeks was too short to jump into a relationship.

Despite all his solid reasons for leaving, he said, "I'd love a cup of hot chocolate."

"Great. I'll go in and get it started while you put the sled in the garage."

She was gone before he could say anything more. He put the sled away and entered the back door that led into her kitchen. Christy already had the hot chocolate on the stove and was stirring it. To his disappointment, she'd pinned up her hair.

He hung up his coat on a nearby chair and stood against the counter. "That looks good."

"It'll taste better," she said. "Would you like a sandwich? I've got tons of cold cuts in the refrigerator."

"I'm fine."

"How about some cake?"

"Christy, I'm fine. We just ate a huge meal, remember?"

"Yeah," Christy replied, trying to concentrate on her chore but feeling excruciatingly conscious of Adam's every move. It was crazy, but when they'd been in the close confines of the car, she'd felt relatively relaxed. Now that they were standing in her kitchen, the sexual tension she had sensed flowing between them all day coalesced inside her into a hard, tight knot of need. She wanted him so badly that her body ached.

Sensing her agitation, Adam frowned. When she'd climbed out of the car she'd seemed fine, and he flipped back through their conversation to see if he'd said or done something that might have upset her.

Unable to come up with anything, he stepped behind her and began massaging the taut muscles in her neck and shoulders. "What's wrong, Christy?"

She flexed beneath his touch like a responsive cat. "Nothing's wrong."

"Then why are you as tight as a bowstring?"

"I'm always like this after an active day."

"Relax," he ordered, increasing the pressure of his fingers.

"Do you want marshmallows?" she asked. If she didn't escape his touch, she was going to melt right at his feet.

"If you have them."

She stepped away from him, opened the cupboard and retrieved a bag of miniature marshmallows. Adam watched her as she poured the hot chocolate into mugs. For once, her expression was impossible to read.

"Are you sure you don't want some cake?" she inquired, handing him a mug.

"I'm sure," he answered, noting that she was refusing to look at him. "Christy, did I say or do something to offend you?"

"Of course not," she said too quickly for Adam's peace of mind.

"Well, if I didn't offend you, then why are you acting as if I'm going to bite you?"

"Because I'm afraid you won't," she returned, boldly raising her eyes to his. "I want you to make love to me so badly that I'm burning up inside."

The flare of desire that shot through Adam at her words was so intense that he nearly doubled over from its onslaught. But he couldn't give in to it. He wasn't ready to leap from heated kisses to making love—that would be committing to a relationship with a woman he barely knew. He'd made that mistake with Andrea, and he wasn't about to repeat it.

"Christy, I told you this afternoon that I'm not ready for that big a step. We need more time to get to know each other. We need to know that what we're doing is right for both of us. Making love would only confuse us, because we wouldn't be approaching our relationship from a logical standpoint."

"Relationships aren't based on logic," Christy argued in frustration. "They're based on feelings, and what I'm feeling for you is so powerful it's frightening. It's also the most exhilarating sensation I've ever experienced in my life. I don't want to analyze it. I want to react."

"And you could be reacting your way right into a broken heart!" he exclaimed heatedly. "I'm a busy man, Christy. I work seven days a week, sixteen-to-eighteen hours a day. I'm willing to make time to date you, but I don't have the time needed to devote to a lover."

When she opened her mouth to respond, he held up a hand for silence. "At first you'd be understanding, because everything would be new and exciting for you. But as time passed, you'd become upset when I wasn't there when you wanted me there, or when something came up and I simply forgot you. I've been there, Christy, and I know what I'm talking about. I have a demanding mistress, and that mistress is work."

He braced himself for her argument, but instead of disagreeing with him, she said, "You'd better drink your hot chocolate before it gets cold."

Adam regarded her warily as she lifted her mug to her lips and took a long sip. He mimicked the action, though the liquid was tasteless as it slid down his throat. What was she thinking? Why didn't she say something? And, dammit, why did she always respond in the opposite manner to what he expected?

Christy worked her way through his impassioned speech, her mind halting at the same spot over and over again. *I've been there, Christy, and I know what I'm talking about.*

Finally the meaning of what he was saying hit her. Adam wasn't worried about breaking her heart. He was worried about getting his own heart broken! That realization filled her with relief, because he wouldn't be worried about a broken heart if he didn't have strong feelings for her. Somehow, she was going to have to find a way to slip behind his self-protective barrier and make him face his feelings. Once she'd accomplished that task, then their relationship could assume its normal course.

But how could she make him understand that she was willing to accommodate his work schedule as long as he made time for her? Not by arguing with him, she assured herself. Anyone as determined to protect himself as Adam was would have rehearsed his position so many times that he'd be able to dispute any contention she presented. The best way to deal with him, she supposed, would be to pretend that she had accepted his terms.

"You're right, Adam," she said at last. "We shouldn't rush into anything. Would you like your hot chocolate warmed up?"

Adam was so stunned by her acquiescence that he could only stare at her. To his chagrin, he was also piqued. Ever since he'd met her she'd been practically throwing herself at him, and now she was dismissing him with a casualness that was downright irksome.

He was tempted to cross the short distance between them and kiss her until she was begging him to make love to her, but he knew he'd only be defeating himself. He'd made his position clear, and now he had to stand behind it.

He drained his mug, set it on the counter and said, "No, thanks. I'd better get to the mall and see if anything urgent happened while I was gone."

"I understand," Christy answered so cheerfully that Adam became even more irked.

He jerked his coat off the chair and pulled it on. "Thanks for taking me sledding."

"Anytime. Thanks for dinner."

"Sure. We'll have to do it again, soon."

"I'd enjoy that."

He shifted from one foot to the other, trying to decide if a good-night kiss was in order. After all, they were going to continue dating. They just weren't going to leap into bed. Under the circumstances, however, he decided to let her make the first move.

"Well, I guess I should say good-night."

"Good night," Christy replied without moving an inch. "Drive carefully."

"Yeah." When she still didn't move, he said, "Well, I'll see you tomorrow."

She only nodded, so he headed for the door. He was halfway there when she spoke. "Adam, didn't you forget something?"

"What?" he asked, spinning around to face her, then freezing as he watched her lift her hands to her hair and release the pins. It fell in a silken cascade over her shoulders and breasts, and he gulped as he watched its descent.

"I'm used to my dates giving me a good-night kiss," she announced in a sultry voice as she walked toward him. "You are going to give me a good-night kiss, aren't you?"

As he watched the provocative sway of her hips, his common sense told him to turn on his heel and run. But no matter how hard he tried, he couldn't move his legs.

When she reached him and laid a hand against his chest, part of his body went weak while the other part went hard.

He wasn't going to make love to her, he told himself firmly. He wasn't! But he couldn't stop himself from re-arranging the locks of her hair that rested against her breasts, nor could he stop himself from letting his fingers slide through the fine, silken strands.

"I've never seen anything so beautiful," he whispered hoarsely.

Christy was afraid to speak. She could sense him warring with his desire, and she knew that if she pushed, she could probably seduce him into her bed. However, if she seduced him, when it was over he'd pull even further away. From here on, anything that happened between them would have to be because he had taken the first step.

She closed her eyes as he once again slid his fingers through her hair, his hands brushing lightly against the crests of her breasts as he reached the ends. She could feel her nipples hardening and fought against the urge to press them into his palms.

Just when she was certain he was never going to kiss her, he caught her chin and tilted her head upward. She parted her lips on a sigh when his mouth moved lazily across hers. When he nipped lightly at her lower lip, she pushed her hands up his chest and wound her arms around his neck. He slid his tongue tentatively into her mouth, and she let her tongue caress his just as tentatively. She was rewarded with his groan as he swept her up against him.

A wild longing surged through her, and she tried to burrow closer to him, but his parka was bunched between them and kept her from molding intimately against him. She wanted to test his response—feel his heat—and she murmured in protest when as she tried to tug his coat out of the way, he caught her hand and brought it up to his chest.

He was breathing shallowly when he slid his lips to her ear and rasped, "What are you going to do if I sweep you into my arms and carry you off to bed?"

"Hope that we never make it that far," she answered breathlessly, and then gasped when he jerked his coat out of the way, grasped her hip and brought her into contact with his erection. Her knees went weak and she began to tremble with need.

"This is crazy," he mumbled as he moved against her. "If I had any sense at all, I'd turn tail and run."

"If you did, I'd run after you. I'm so hot inside, Adam, that I'm going to burst into flame if you don't make love to me."

"How far is your bedroom?" he whispered harshly as he swung her up into his arms.

"Miles."

"Then give me a kiss so I'll have enough strength to get there."

She obeyed his command, and when she lifted her lips from his, he was already at the top of the stairs.

7

"ARE YOU SURE this is what you want?" Adam asked as he carried Christy into her bedroom. "If it's not, honey, then tell me now, because I'm on the edge of no return."

"I'm sure," she said. "Make love to me, Adam."

He lowered her to the bed and came down over her. Christy had never felt this urgency to possess or to be possessed, and she slid her hand between them and began to stroke Adam's penis. She groaned in frustration when he captured her hand and anchored it to the bed.

"You have to slow down," he murmured as he raised his head and smiled tautly. "If you don't, the fireworks are going to go off before we're even undressed, and then what good am I going to be to you?"

Her impatience faded at his words. She still wanted him—wouldn't be satisfied until they'd made love—but they had all night. She laughed as she wrapped her arms around his neck, pulling him down for a slow, languorous kiss.

"What's the joke?" he asked when she finally let him come up for air.

"No joke. I'm just happy." She pushed his jacket off his shoulders. "I'm also glad we aren't playing strip poker. We're wearing so many clothes that it would take us all night to get undressed."

"Well, I agree that sledding clothes definitely make seduction hard work, but it can also heighten the anticipation, so let's handle this a piece of clothing at a time."

"Sounds like a good plan to me," she said after he stole another kiss and then sat on the edge of the bed and removed his jacket.

He brushed his knuckles against her cheek before pulling her up beside him and reaching for the hem of her sweatshirt. They kissed before she removed his sweatshirt. Then they kissed again after removing the tops of their long underwear. Christy took advantage of the opportunity to caress his bare chest as he released the clasp of her bra and slid it down her arms. He was such a tantalizing contrast of textures that her senses were almost overloaded.

Adam shuddered in pleasure beneath Christy's exploring touch, and he gently, reverently, pressed the tips of his fingers to the roseate peaks of her breasts. She was so small, yet so sexy, and he spread her hair over her shoulders, brushing the tip of a trailing tendril over one nipple.

Christy closed her eyes and caught her lower lip between her teeth to hold back the moan of pleasure that arose when he laved his tongue over the sensitive peak. Her sense of urgency returned in full force as he teased at the other breast, and she tried to use the relaxation techniques she'd learned over the years. She wanted to prolong this first time, to experience it to its fullest—but already, her control was waning.

Her stomach muscles clenched beneath the touch of his fingers as he laid her back on the bed, opening the snap of her denims and lowered the zipper. He eased them off, and she smiled ruefully as she reflected that the bottoms of her long underwear could hardly be considered seductive. But when she glanced at Adam through her lashes, he was gazing down at her as if she wore gossamer lingerie.

Slowly, temptingly, he removed the remainder of her clothing. Her breath caught in her throat as he trailed his fingers from her waist to her ankles, before retracing his journey, lingering at her inner thighs. Then, pressing the heel of his hand against her apex, he curled his fingers into the fine golden curls there.

Christy tensed, waiting for the magic touch that his hold promised, and her eyes opened when he said, "Christy, are you protected?"

"No," she groaned miserably as she tossed her arm over her eyes. "I should have had the foresight to pick up something, but—"

"Shh," Adam whispered as he drew her arm away from her face and pressed a feather-light kiss to her hot cheek. "I'm prepared."

She watched as he fished his wallet out of his pocket, retrieved a foil packet and set it on the bedside table. Then he stood and removed the remainder of his clothes. He was so beautiful that Christy simply stared.

"Are you okay?" he asked as he joined her on the bed.

"I'm wonderful," she answered, and the time for words was over.

They tasted and teased with their hands and their lips until Christy was sure she'd explode if he didn't come to her. She wrapped her legs around his hips and arched upward, letting out a gasp of pleasurable surprise when he surged into her.

Adam let out his own gasp. She was so soft and hot and tight that he nearly came. Breathing deeply, he fought for control. But he couldn't remain still for long, and he began to rock against her slowly, gazing into her face. He'd always considered her beautiful, but she was exquisite with her eyes glowing with passion and her skin flushed. As his movements became more demanding and

WOW!

THE MOST GENEROUS
FREE OFFER EVER!

From the Harlequin Reader Service®

GET 4 FREE BOOKS WORTH MORE THAN $11.00

Affix peel-off stickers to reply card

FOUR FREE BOOKS

FOUR FREE BOOKS

PLUS A FREE VICTORIAN PICTURE FRAME

AND A FREE MYSTERY GIFT!

NO COST! NO OBLIGATION TO BUY!
NO PURCHASE NECESSARY!

Because you're a reader of Harlequin romances, the publishers would like you to accept four brand-new Harlequin Temptation® novels, with their compliments. Accepting this offer places you under no obligation to purchase any books, ever!

ACCEPT FOUR BRAND-NEW

YOURS

We'd like to send you four free Harlequin novels, worth more than $11.00, to introduce you to the benefits of the Harlequin Reader Service®. We hope your free books will convince you to subscribe, but that's up to you. Accepting them places you under no obligation to buy anything, but we hope you'll want to continue with the Reader Service.

So unless we hear from you, once a month, we'll send you 4 additional Harlequin Temptation® novels to read and enjoy. If you choose to keep them, you'll pay just $2.69* per volume—a saving of 30¢ each off the cover price. There is no charge for shipping and handling. There are no hidden extras! And you may cancel at any time, for any reason, just by sending us a note or a shipping statement marked "cancel." You can even return any shipment to us at our expense. Either way, the free books and gifts are yours to keep!

ALSO FREE!
VICTORIAN PICTURE FRAME

This lovely Victorian pewter-finish miniature is perfect for displaying a treasured photograph—and it's yours *absolutely free*—when you accept our no-risk offer.

Perfect for a treasured Photograph

Plus a FREE mystery Gift follow instructions at right.

*Terms and prices subject to change without notice. Sales taxes applicable in NY.

© 1990 Harlequin Enterprises Limited

HARLEQUIN TEMPTATION® NOVELS
FREE!

Harlequin Reader Service®

```
AFFIX
FOUR FREE BOOKS
STICKER HERE
```

YES, send me my four free books and gifts as
explained on the opposite page. I have affixed my
"free books" sticker above and my two "free gift"
stickers below. I understand that accepting these
books and gifts places me under no obligation ever to
buy any books; I may cancel at any time, for any reason,
and the free books and gifts will be mine to keep!

142 CIH ADNH
(U-H-T-12/91)

NAME _____

(PLEASE PRINT)

ADDRESS _____ APT. ____

CITY _____

STATE _____ ZIP _____

Offer limited to one per household and not valid to current Harlequin Temptation® subscribers. All orders
subject to approval.

```
AFFIX FREE
VICTORIAN
PICTURE
FRAME
STICKER HERE
```

```
AFFIX FREE
MYSTERY GIFT
STICKER HERE
```

© 1990 HARLEQUIN ENTERPRISES LIMITED

PRINTED IN U.S.A.

WE EVEN PROVIDE FREE POSTAGE!

It costs you *nothing* to send for your free books — we've paid the postage on the attached reply card. And we'll pick up the postage on your shipment of free books and gifts, and also on any subsequent shipments of books, should you choose to become a subscriber. Unlike many book clubs, we charge *nothing* for postage and handling!

DETACH AND RETURN TODAY

HARLEQUIN READER SERVICE
3010 WALDEN AVE
PO BOX 1867
BUFFALO NY 14240-9952

POSTAGE WILL BE PAID BY ADDRESSEE

BUSINESS REPLY MAIL
FIRST CLASS MAIL   PERMIT NO. 717   BUFFALO, NY

NO POSTAGE
NECESSARY
IF MAILED
IN THE
UNITED STATES

she met him thrust for thrust, giving as he gave, Adam knew that lovemaking had never been so good for him. When she climaxed, shuddering in his arms and bringing him to the most explosive orgasm he'd ever experienced, he also knew that he was in love with her. It was crazy. Absolutely insane. It was impossible to fall in love in five days, but he had.

"That was so wonderful. So beautiful. So sensational," she said on a sigh as he rolled to his side and brought her with him.

"It was every one of those things and more," Adam whispered as he buried his fingers in her hair and massaged her scalp.

She sighed again, resting her head against his shoulder, her fingers toying with the hair on his chest. A few minutes later, they stilled, and Adam knew she'd fallen asleep.

It was only then that he allowed himself to explore his feelings for her, prodding at them and testing them. And still he reached the same conclusion. He was in love with her, and he didn't know what to do about it. As he'd told her today, they were too different. And he knew from firsthand experience that even love couldn't resolve differences. Look at his parents. Look at his father and stepmother. Look at what had happened between him and Andrea.

If he was smart, he'd end everything now and never see her again, but as he brushed Christy's hair away from her face and watched her sleep, he knew he couldn't just walk away after making love with her. It would hurt her, and he'd never be able to live with himself if he hurt her. He'd have to hang in there, and when she finally saw that they were simply too different to make a go of it, she'd walk away from him.

It would hurt, he admitted as he rubbed his cheek against her hair, but at least he'd have his work to help ease him through the pain. In the meantime, he'd enjoy their time together.

CHRISTY AWOKE AT DAWN. It took her a moment to orient herself to the warm body lying beside her, and when she did, she blushed in memory of the night she'd shared with Adam. They'd made love, slept for a while, and then made love again. Unbelievably, the second time had been even better.

She shifted so she could look at his sleeping face. How could anyone look so delicious in the morning? She wanted to reach out and touch his morning beard, but she knew that it was rare for him to get a good night's sleep. Instead she lay quietly beside him, content to watch him. She was in love with him, and after last night, she believed that if Adam wasn't in love with her, it would only be a matter of time before he was. A man didn't make love to a woman the way he had and not have special feelings. She smiled at the thought.

"How can you possibly be grinning so early in the morning?" Adam asked with a sleepy yawn and a full-body stretch that Christy found delightfully erotic.

"I'm not grinning, I'm smiling," she told him as he rolled onto his side so that he was facing her.

"And what are you smiling about?" he asked huskily as he wrapped an arm around her and pulled her against him.

"Probably the same thing you're smiling about," she murmured, touching a finger to the upward curve of his lips. "You have such a nice smile. It's too bad you don't use it more often."

He pressed a kiss to her fingertip. "If I did that, I might wear it out."

"Nope. Smiles get better with use."

"Mmm." He hugged her closer. "How about a good-morning kiss?"

"I don't know," she teased, shivering in delight as she felt him growing hard against her abdomen. She caressed the soft flesh of his taut buttocks before sliding her hand between them to stroke his penis. "I'm not sure I'd be satisfied with a kiss, and you said you wanted to get to the office by six. If you don't want to be late . . ."

"I'm the boss. I can be late if I want, and I want," he said with a groan as she began to stroke him more boldly.

"Me, too," Christy whispered when he slid his fingers between her thighs. His feather-light touch made her contract in a spasm of desire that was almost painful, and she tried to shift away from his hand.

"Don't fight it, honey," Adam told her, rolling her to her back and tossing his leg over hers to stop her efforts to escape. "Go with it, Christy. Relax and go with it."

"Relax?" She gasped as she gripped his shoulders, needing to anchor herself; she was reeling.

"That's it, sweetheart," Adam encouraged as she began to pant. "Just let it happen."

That was easy for him to say! Christy thought as she closed her eyes and cried out softly at the pleasurable pain pulsing through her. She was on the edge of orgasm, but she teetered on the brink before finally crying out, "Oh, Adam!" when she came.

"You are so beautiful," Adam rasped as he entered her quickly, urgently, letting out a groan as her body tightened around him in welcome. "So beautiful, so beautiful."

Christy had never felt such an all-consuming passion as he moved inside her, once again sending her careening toward ecstasy. She wrapped her legs around his waist and curled her fingers into the muscles of his back as she met him thrust for thrust, straining toward climax. And then he tossed back his head and made one final thrust that plummeted them both into instant release.

When Adam collapsed against her, she clung to him. There were no words to explain what she was feeling, so she didn't even try. Instead she caressed him and kissed him, and cuddled against him when he rolled to his side and brought her with him, running his hands soothingly over her body.

Adam would have been content to lie with her like this forever, but the alarm clock went off, reminding him that he had a mall to take care of. With reluctance he let Christy turn away from him to shut off the alarm.

"Too bad we can't make time stand still for a while," she told him as she sat up, raking her hand through her tangled hair. "What would you like for breakfast?"

"I don't have time for breakfast," Adam replied as he slid out of bed and began to gather his clothes from the floor. "I have to get home, shower and shave and get to work. I've been away from the mall since noon yesterday. No telling what disasters await me."

Christy watched him dress. He'd gone from tender lover to workaholic in the blink of an eye. "You should eat breakfast, Adam. It isn't healthy to skip meals, particularly when you work as hard as you do."

"I'll pick up something at the mall," he said as he stretched across the bed and dropped a quick kiss to her lips. "See you later."

"Maybe we can have lunch together," she suggested.

"Mmm. We'll see. I'll have to check my schedule," he answered as he went toward the door. "I'll let you know."

He was gone before Christy could respond, and she picked up her pillow and tossed it at the empty doorway in a fit of temper. She knew she was being childish, but as far as she was concerned, she was completely justified in her behavior. The least he could have done was act as if he wanted to have lunch with her, particularly after they'd just made such fantastic love.

Maybe her father was right. Maybe Adam was a hopeless cause. Maybe she shouldn't be wasting her time on him. Maybe she should tell him to tuck his mall into his back pocket and take a hike.

She groaned when she threw herself down on the bed and inhaled Adam's musky scent, which evoked memories of their lovemaking. She closed her eyes and shook her head in weary resignation. She shouldn't expect miracles overnight. And in all fairness to Adam, he had warned her that it would be this way, so she had no right to complain. Instead, she had to be patient and understanding.

Sighing, she climbed out of bed and headed for the shower. Why did love have to be so darned complicated?

CHRISTY HAD HOPED to get to the mall early enough to see Adam before she started her day, but their sledding trip yesterday and their lovemaking last night had put her behind schedule. She'd spent three hours developing photographs and still hadn't accomplished as much as she'd hoped.

As she walked to the storage room where she kept her camera equipment, she glanced at her watch. She had just enough time to get set up before the mall opened.

Her father rarely arrived until moments before the doors opened, and she let out a yelp of surprise when she hurried into the booth and nearly tripped over his feet. The fact that he'd entered the booth without her there to protect him from the reindeer didn't bode well.

"Good morning, Pop," she said with forced cheerfulness. Surprised, she noted he was furious. For a moment she was at a loss as to why, but the answer was quick in coming. Her parents lived two doors down from her. Her father was an early riser. Adam hadn't left until after the sun had come up. She didn't need to be a mathematical genius to solve the equation, and she cursed the embarrassed blush that heated her cheeks.

He crossed his arms over his chest and glared at her defiantly. "What's good about it?"

"Well, the sun's shining and the predictions are for fair weather," she replied, keeping it light. "That's good for business, and I need all the business I can get if I'm going to keep up my mortgage payments."

"Maybe you should get a second job," he suggested with a barely concealed sneer that rankled, but Christy told herself to maintain her cool. He was trying to get a rise out of her, and she wasn't going to take the bait. Why had she bought a house so close to her parents? Because it had been large enough to accommodate her studio, which saved her office rent, and because she'd wanted to be nearby so she could keep a careful watch on them. Since she hadn't been involved with anyone at the time, she hadn't considered the complications of taking a lover.

"Don't be ridiculous, Pop," she said as she unfolded her tripod. "You know I spend half the night developing photographs in order to meet my five-day delivery schedule. I don't have time for a second job."

"You don't have time for a second job, but you do have time to pussyfoot around with Adam Worth? You'd be better off with a second job."

"You may be right," Christy responded as she loaded a fresh roll of film into her camera. "But as you've told me so many times over the years, all work and no play gives a person ulcers. You don't want me to have ulcers, do you?"

Robert bounded out of his chair and began to pace the booth. "Dammit, Christmas! The man is going to break your heart!"

"He might," she agreed. "And if he does, then you have my permission to say 'I told you so.' But until that happens, I'd appreciate it if you'd keep your thoughts to yourself."

"You're just like your mother," he accused. "She never listens to me, either, and it drives me crazy."

Christy smothered a grin. "It can't be that bad, Pop. You've been married to Mom for forty-nine years and the doctors haven't committed you yet."

"You're so damn stubborn!"

Christy raised her head from her task to look at him. "Well, I should hope so. I am my father's daughter, and it wouldn't be fair if I'd inherited all my personality traits from Mom."

Robert snatched his Santa hat from his head and slapped it against his thigh. "What in the world do you see in him?"

"Outside of the normal man-woman things, I think I like Adam because he reminds me of you." She chuckled when he stared at her in openmouthed shock. "You'd better close your mouth before your dentures fall out."

"You know perfectly well that every tooth in my mouth is my own," he groused. "And what do you mean he reminds you of me? I'm not anything like Adam Worth!"

"Oh, but you are," Christy said. "You're both determined to tell me what's best for me instead of letting me make my own decisions. Believe it or not, Pop, I had a heck of a time convincing Adam to see me. I don't think he's any more comfortable with the situation than you are, but I'm not going to let the two of you dictate my life.

"I know Adam will be courteous to you," she continued before he could respond, "and I expect you to be courteous to him. If you don't think you can do that, please tell me now."

"And if I say I can't?" he challenged.

"Then this will be a part of my life that I won't share with you. I don't want to shut you out, but I will if I have to," Christy replied, quietly but firmly.

Robert dropped back into his chair, his shoulders slumped in defeat. "I'll be nice to him."

"I knew you would," Christy urged as she went to him, hugging him tightly and blinking against a sudden surge of tears. "I love you, Pop, and I know you only want to protect me, but I have to live my life the way that I feel is best for me."

"I know that," Robert stated gruffly as he gave her an awkward hug in return. "Now, you'd better get back to your camera. They're going to open the doors any minute."

Christy nodded and pulled away, swiping at her teary eyes. She hated confrontations with either of her parents. All her life they'd been there for her, protecting her and supporting her; but when her father had fallen ill, she'd had to come face-to-face with their mortality. As she'd told Adam yesterday, she had to stand on her own two feet and take responsibility for her actions, because one day her parents wouldn't be there to help her through the rough times.

The thought might have sent her plunging into the pits of depression if she hadn't looked up and seen Adam striding toward the booth. She raced down the corridor to meet him. Her father had promised to be polite, but since he was probably still smarting from losing their argument, she didn't think it prudent to put him to the test.

"Good morning, handsome," she said when she reached him. "Got a kiss for a pair of lonesome lips?"

"I have a peck," Adam replied, treating her to one. "If you want more, you'll have to wait until we're alone. It's not polite to give public displays of affection."

"I should have known that you'd be a stickler for etiquette," Christy remarked, grinning up at him. "So, when can I get you alone?"

Adam gave a resigned shake of his head. "I'm afraid that I have back-to-back appointments today and a dinner engagement tonight that I can't get out of. Let's meet for breakfast tomorrow."

Christy hesitated. He had a dinner engagement? She wanted to ask with whom, but she was too afraid it was with another woman. When she felt the stirring of jealousy, she forced it down. If Adam was having dinner with another woman, he'd made the plans before last night. It would be rude to cancel at the last minute, and she knew in her heart that dinner was all he'd be sharing. She trusted him completely when it came to fidelity. What worried her, however, was that the woman was most likely older and far more sophisticated than she was. Adam had already indicated that her age bothered him. If he started to compare her to one of his contemporaries, would she measure up?

"Why don't you stop by after dinner?" she ventured with a bright smile that she hoped didn't look as false as it felt. "I'll be working until the wee hours, but I can take time out for a coffee break."

Adam was tempted to accept her invitation, but he shook his head, because he knew they wouldn't stop at coffee. He'd end up spending another night in her bed, and as tempting as that sounded, one look at his In-Box this morning had been enough to tell him that he'd have to burn the midnight oil if he hoped to catch up.

"I'm sorry, Christy, but I can't. I'm going to have to come back to the mall after dinner. Maybe tomorrow night."

Christy would have been far more reassured if he'd made a definite commitment for tomorrow night, but she told herself not to push. "Then I guess I'll see you tomorrow morning for breakfast. Is eight okay?"

"I'll make sure it's okay. Do you want to meet at the booth?"

Christy stepped close to him and rubbed her hand up and down his lapel. "Let's meet in your office," she murmured suggestively. "As you said, it isn't polite to make public displays of affection, and by then I'll be in need of some heavy affection."

Desire flared in Adam at the provocative glow in her eyes, and he wanted to sweep her up into his arms and take her somewhere where he could make passionate love to her. "My office, it is."

"Eight sharp," Christy replied as she watched a flurry of emotions race across his face—emotions that left no doubt in her mind that he was as affected by her presence as she was by his. She was tempted to drag him into the nearest supply closet and have her way with him, but her father chose that moment to yell that it was time to go to work. With a sigh, she rose on tiptoe and gave Adam a quick kiss. "I'd better get back to the booth. Duty calls."

"Sounds more like Santa to me," Adam remarked, glancing cautiously in Robert's direction. If the man even suspected what was going on between him and his daughter, he'd probably be gunning for him.

"Don't worry about Pop," Christy said as she followed his gaze. "He knows all about us, and he's accepted it."

"He accepted us dating just like that?" he asked skeptically.

"In a manner of speaking," Christy hedged.

"Christy—" Adam began, but Robert called again and she dashed off.

Adam stuffed his hands in his pockets and frowned as he watched her enter the booth. The first customers of the day arrived just seconds after she did, and he continued to watch as she and Robert settled into their routine, trying to guess what, exactly, had transpired between father and daughter.

But unless he were to interrupt her work, which he wasn't about to do, he'd have to wait until they were alone to discuss the issue. And they would discuss it. Christy and Robert had the type of relationship he'd always longed to have with his own father, and he'd never forgive himself if he caused a rift between them.

The thought made his frown deepen as he returned to his office. He was having dinner with his father and stepmother tonight, and he wasn't looking forward to the gathering. Marsha had mellowed toward him over the years, but he still felt as if he were an intruder in her home, and he couldn't figure out why his father insisted he come to dinner once a month. They were so uncomfortable with one another that they never discussed more than each other's health, the weather and the mall.

When he reached his office and was faced with his overflowing In-tray, he was tempted to cancel dinner, but even as he reached for the telephone, he knew he couldn't do it. He'd already managed to avoid Thanksgiving dinner, and he'd promised his father that he'd make it tonight. Canceling out at the last minute would not only be rude; it would irritate the hell out of Marsha, who didn't like her plans disrupted. He'd lived away from his family for eighteen years, so he could remove himself from their arguments, and he wasn't about to do anything that would return him to the old status quo.

He leaned back in his chair and closed his eyes with a weary sigh. Why had he come back to Colorado Springs? Why hadn't he opened his mall in China or Greenland or Borneo? At least there, he would have continued to have the excuse of distance to stay away. So why had he come back?

Because for better or worse, his family was all he had, and he'd been tired of being alone.

When he felt the familiar depression descending, he shoved it aside. He was too busy to be depressed. Besides, he wasn't the only person in the world to come from a dysfunctional family. In fact, he'd be willing to bet that ninety-nine percent of families were dysfunctional in one way or another. The Christy Knights of the world were the exception rather than the rule. Which once again made him ask himself what was drawing her to him.

Was she looking for a father figure? He recalled her revelation about her father's heart attack. He knew it wasn't unusual for a child raised by older parents to be attracted to a more mature person. Since she'd been forced to come face-to-face with her father's mortality, she might be seeking someone she felt could fill the gap once he was gone.

But even as Adam considered that possibility, something inside him balked at it. Christy was one of the most strong-willed women he'd ever met. She seemed to know exactly what she wanted and wasn't afraid to go after it. That didn't fit the personality of a woman who needed a father figure. Which brought him back to square one. What *did* she see in him?

Unfortunately, only she knew the answer. He'd worry about it when he didn't have so much work to do.

IT HAD BEEN THE MOST hectic day Christy and her father had had to date, and she was emotionally drained when quitting time finally rolled around. Her father had left for home, and though she knew she had a ton of photographs to develop and should head for home herself, she needed to take some time to relax.

She resisted the urge to wander up to Adam's office and see if he was in. She didn't want to be a pest, but he'd only stopped by the booth twice today, and both times she'd been so busy that she hadn't been able to give him more than a quick hello. She wished she'd been able to ask how his day was going. She wished they'd been able to spend some time together, even if it was only for a few minutes. She wished she knew who his dinner engagement was with. She wished . . .

She wished she'd stop wishing. And she was going to do exactly that. She strolled through the mall, stopping every now and then to look at something in a window that caught her eye. Normally, window-shopping soothed her, but tonight she needed something more challenging to occupy her troubled mind.

When she neared the video-game arcade, she knew she'd found the antidote, and she dug into the pocket of her costume and pulled out a five-dollar bill. It would supply her with more than enough quarters to kill a good hour, and then she'd go home and get to work. She entered the arcade, got her quarters, and then perused the room, trying to decide which game she wanted to tackle first.

"Hey, shouldn't you be at the North Pole making toys and loading Santa's sleigh," a young voice drawled.

Christy looked over her shoulder to discover a redheaded boy of about fifteen grinning at her.

"I'm Santa's research assistant," she explained, grinning back. "My assignment tonight is to check out video games. Any suggestions on where I should start?"

He stuffed his hands into his pockets and swaggered toward her. "That depends. You a beginner?"

"Expert," Christy told him.

"Yeah? Interested in a match?"

Christy assessed him. She'd been champion of her neighborhood arcade back in Philadelphia, but she hadn't played since she'd come home. The confident gleam in the boy's eyes told her he'd be a tough opponent, and the competitor in her surfaced.

"Best two games out of three," she said. "What'll we play for?"

"A buck a game?" he suggested slyly.

Christy laughed. "No way. That's gambling, and not only is gambling illegal in this state, I could be arrested for contributing to the delinquency of a minor. How about a burrito and a cola at Bertha's Mexican Hat?"

Rubbing his hands together in anticipation, he said, "Let's get this match on the road. I'm starving!"

ADAM WAS RUNNING behind schedule. He rushed through the mall, debating whether he should phone his father and tell him he might be late for dinner. He had planned on getting out of the office early, but just when he'd been ready to call it a day, Security had notified him there was a potential crowd-control problem at the video-game arcade. At first he'd been tempted to tell them to handle it on their own, but then decided to check it out. The last thing he wanted at this point in time was bad publicity.

"What's going on?" he yelled at one of the security guards when he arrived at the arcade just as a roaring cheer erupted. There were so many kids packed into the room that he couldn't see what was happening.

"Championship game!" the guard yelled back. "It's been going on for close to an hour, and both players have already beat the record. As soon as the word got out, every teenager in the mall showed up to watch the action."

"Damn," Adam muttered as he tried to spot the center of their attention. He knew that malls had become the "in" place for teenagers to hang out, and generally they didn't cause much trouble. But whenever this many congregated in one spot, the situation was potentially explosive.

His jaw dropped when he realized that one of the players involved in the "championship game" was dressed as an elf. It couldn't be Christy! Unable to decide whether he should be amused or angry, he just shook his head and smiled as he watched her. Ten minutes passed before the game ended, and Adam wasn't sure who'd won until Christy raised the boy's arm into the air as if proclaiming the victor of a boxing match. The cheering was so loud it was almost deafening. When the noise lowered a few decibels, she began to wend her way through the crowd, accepting condolences while her competitor trailed after her, accepting congratulations. She was so involved with the teenagers that she would have passed Adam by if he hadn't stepped in front of her.

"Adam!" she exclaimed in surprised delight. "What are you doing here?"

"Working crowd control," he answered as he cast a meaningful glance around them. "You caused a potential riot situation."

Christy grinned up at him. "They'll break up as soon as I haul away the victor."

"Haul away the victor?"

"The loser has to treat the winner to a burrito and a cola at Bertha's Mexican Hat. Want to join us?"

"I can't," Adam said. "I'm supposed to be at my father's in less than an hour, and if I don't get a move on, I'll be late for dinner."

"Sounds ominous," she commented, feeling an overwhelming sense of relief when she realized that his dinner engagement was a family affair. She also tucked the information away as she took note of his dry tone. Something told her that she should do a little delving into the Worth family tree, because every time Adam mentioned his father he became tense.

"It is ominous," he replied. "My stepmother doesn't like to be kept waiting, so I'd better run. I'll see you tomorrow morning."

Christy nodded. He turned to walk away, but suddenly stopped and faced her. "Sorry you lost the game."

She shrugged. "I'll win next time."

The confidence in her voice and the mischief in her eyes clued Adam in. "You let that kid win, didn't you?"

Her smile was devilish. "Adam, how could you even suggest such a thing?"

"Because I can see right through you. Why did you do it?"

"Maybe I'll tell you tomorrow. Right now, I have a burrito to buy, and you have a dinner date with your family. Have a good evening."

Adam reached out and caught her hand. Before she knew what was happening, she was in his arms.

"Why, Mr. Worth, what has gotten into you? Public displays of affection are impolite," she told him with a mock primness that didn't disguise the laughter in her voice.

Adam dropped a quick kiss on her lips and, chuckling, asked, "Why did you let the kid win?"

Christy looked about to make sure they couldn't be heard. "If you were a fifteen-year-old boy, how would you feel if your friends saw you lose to an elf?"

"I'd want the earth to open up and swallow me."

"Exactly."

"So, you did it to spare his ego?"

"No. I did it because his friends would devil the heck out of him, and he could end up with some weird nickname that would stay with him the rest of his life. The next time I play him, I'll be dressed like a normal person, and I'll beat the socks off him," Christy answered.

Adam shook his head as he caught a loose strand of her hair and tucked it beneath her cap. "Why do you always wear your hair up?"

She gave him a bemused look. "Because it keeps it out of my eyes. Why?"

"Because I prefer it down."

"I'll wear it down for you tomorrow morning," she promised, her voice soft and seductive. Then she became brisk. "Now, you'd better get going. You don't want to be ominously late."

Adam knew she was right, but he didn't want to spend the evening making polite conversation with his father and stepmother. He wanted to be with Christy. He wanted her to wear her hair down for him tonight. He wanted to know how her day had gone—everything, including the smallest mundane detail.

As if sensing his reluctance to leave, she backed out of his embrace and repeated, "You'd better get going, Adam. You're going to be late."

Adam watched as she rounded up the boy from the arcade and led him toward Bertha's Mexican Hat. Just before she disappeared from sight, she glanced over her shoulder and winked at him. If anyone had told him that such a simple act could make him feel so warm inside, he wouldn't have believed them.

"Well, I think everything's over now, Mr. Worth," the security guard stated as he walked out of the arcade.

No, Adam answered inwardly. *I think everything has just begun.*

8

"ADAM! COME IN!" Charles Worth greeted with what sounded to Adam like forced joviality when he opened the door.

"Hello, Dad," he said as he entered the house. As usual, he was faced with that awkward moment of indecision over whether to shake hands with his father or hug him. Since his father seemed just as indecisive, he extended his hand. "I hope I'm not late."

"Actually, you're right on time. I'm afraid Marsha and I are running a little behind, though. We, uh, got tied up and forgot about the time. How about a drink?"

"No, thanks. The streets are icy, so I'd better stick to coffee." Adam followed his father into the living room, eyeing him warily. He'd swear his father had blushed when he'd said he and Marsha had gotten tied up and forgot about the time. He suspected they'd had another row. Hopefully it wasn't about him coming to dinner.

"It's damn cold outside," he remarked as he took a seat on the sofa.

"It sure is, and according to the weatherman, it's going to stay that way for a few days. At least it's too cold to snow, so we'll be spared that mess for a while," Charles responded as he settled into his favorite reclining chair.

"Amen to that."

"So, how's everything at the mall?"

"Busy and hectic," Adam answered as he glanced around the room. He had to give Marsha credit for her decorating skills—the room was warm and inviting, and his eyes strayed over the many pictures of his half sister, Danielle. "How's Dani feeling?"

"Big as a house," Marsha announced as she walked into the room and set a plate of raw vegetables and a yogurt dip on the coffee table. "But that's to be expected. She is seven months pregnant. How are you, Adam?"

"Fine, Marsha. And you?"

"Just fine."

A strained silence fell over them. Adam searched for some topic of conversation to engage in, but came up blank. He'd already talked about the weather and the mall, so he concentrated on the vegetable plate and dip, finally saying, "This is a wonderful dip, Marsha."

"Thanks. You two enjoy it. I need to get back to dinner."

"Need any help?" Charles asked.

"Not your kind," Marsha said with a wry smile that looked more like a smirk to Adam. "You've already made dinner late, and Adam is probably starving."

"I'm fine, Marsha," Adam assured quickly, ready as always to divert attention away from himself. "I always eat late, if I remember to eat at all, so don't worry about me."

She glanced from him to his father before saying, "As they say, like father like son. You should take better care of yourself, Adam. Dinner will be ready shortly."

When she left the room, Adam said, "If tonight was inconvenient, Dad, you should have called me. We could have rescheduled."

A look of frustration raced through his father's eyes, but it was gone so quickly that Adam thought he'd imagined it.

"It wasn't inconvenient, Adam, and we don't see enough of you as it is. If I didn't know you were so busy, I'd think you were avoiding us."

"Aren't you going to have any dip?" Adam asked, hoping to dodge that sticky wicket as he once again concentrated on the vegetable plate. He couldn't tell his father that he was indeed avoiding them. Yet he couldn't bring himself to lie to him, either.

"Just hand me a piece of celery," his father replied. "I'm trying to lose a few pounds, and they don't drop off as easily as they did at your age."

Adam handed him the celery and reached for a cauliflower floret for himself. He nearly choked on it when Charles inquired, "So, how's your love life?"

It wasn't the first time his father had asked the question, and Adam knew that he was simply making conversation. So why was he uncomfortable with the question? Perhaps it was because he'd never had anything to report before.

"Actually, it's looking up," he said. "I've met a very interesting woman."

"That's great. What's her name?"

Adam smiled. "She goes by Christy, but her name is Christmas. Christmas Knight with a *K*. I think you'd like her. She's very... unusual."

"You'll have to bring her to dinner one night."

Marsha chose that moment to announce that it was time to eat, and Adam was saved from having to respond. The last place he'd ever bring Christy was here. She shared such an open, loving relationship with her father, and he could imagine how horrified she'd be by the stiff formality between him and his father. Good heavens, they couldn't even share a hug!

It was a sobering thought, and Adam experienced a keen pang of sadness as he studied his father across the table. They hadn't always been this distant, though he couldn't pinpoint when the change had begun to occur, or which of them had begun to withdraw first. He would have liked to say it was his father, but there was a part of him, deep down inside, whispering that it might have been himself.

As he took note of his father's graying hair, which was now more silver than brown, and the distinguished character lines that etched his face, he wondered if it was too late for them to regain what they'd once had. Could they reach a point where they could discuss more than each other's health, the weather, and the mall? Could they become friends?

Adam didn't have the answers, but he did know that he wanted to try. The question was, where did he start?

CHRISTY'S HEART SKIPPED a beat when her doorbell rang. She told herself that it wasn't Adam. He'd said he wouldn't be stopping by tonight, and she'd be a fool to think he'd changed his mind. It was probably her mother coming for a visit, or her father coming to give her another lecture. He may have conceded defeat this morning, but it didn't mean that he wouldn't make another pitch.

Just in case it was Adam, however, she made a quick stop at the mirror and released her hair from its ponytail, finger-combing it as she hurried to the door. He'd said he preferred it down, and if that's what he wanted, then that's what he'd get.

"Adam!" she exclaimed breathlessly when she threw open the door. But her excitement turned to confusion when he scowled at her. "What's wrong?"

"You're supposed to find out who's at your door before you open it. Good heavens, Christy! For all you knew, I was the neighborhood ax murderer."

At any other time, Christy might have taken offense at his scolding, but tonight she was too happy to see him. "In the first place, we don't have a neighborhood ax murderer, and in the second place, he wouldn't ring the doorbell. He'd use the key under the doormat."

Adam's gaze automatically dropped to the doormat beneath his feet. "You are joking, aren't you?"

"Of course I'm joking," Christy said with a chuckle. "I'm impulsive, Adam, but I'm not stupid. Are you coming in, or did you just stop by to lecture me?"

His expression became hesitant. "Well, I decided to take you up on your offer of coffee, but if I'm interrupting your work, we can make it another time."

"You're not interrupting. Your timing is perfect—I just closed down the darkroom."

"Well, if you're sure I'm not interrupting," Adam insisted. He shouldn't have stopped by without calling. In fact, considering the state of his office, he shouldn't be here at all. But his visit with his father had depressed him and he'd come to the one person guaranteed to cheer him up.

"Adam, get in here," Christy ordered impatiently as she grabbed his arm and tugged. "All my heat is going outside, and my heating bill is already outrageous."

Adam didn't need any further encouragement, and he stepped inside. Immediately he was greeted with a wolf whistle and a rendition of "Sexy man alert! Sexy man alert!"

"Is that Gypsy's only line?" he asked with a soft laugh when he finally located the parrot, who was perched on a swing in a gigantic and obscenely ornate bird cage.

"She has other lines." She stepped close to him and wrapped her arms around his neck. "Listen."

He laughed again when Gypsy said, "Kiss, kiss, kiss."

"Well, you heard the bird," Christy prompted with a grin. "Kiss, kiss, kiss."

Again, Adam didn't need any further encouragement. He lowered his lips to hers, and as he'd known it would, his depression began to fade. In its place came warmth and comfort, and, of course, desire. But it wasn't urgent passion. It was more like a gentle yearning that rolled through him. When he released her from the kiss, his heart hesitated at the soft glow in her eyes and the tenderness of her smile.

"How about that coffee?" he reminded gruffly as he shucked his topcoat and hung it on the rack next to her door.

"Sure," Christy said as she took his hand and led him toward the back of the house. "But I should warn you that it's decaf."

"Decaf!" he repeated in mock horror. "How am I supposed to get jump-started on decaf?"

"I'm sure we'll figure out a way to get your motor running," she responded with a wicked grin.

The desire that flooded Adam this time wasn't gentle. In fact, he couldn't remember ever becoming so hard so fast. But he didn't reach for Christy, because he wasn't mentally ready to make love. He wanted to sit with her, visit with her and learn more about her; he couldn't think of a more stimulating kind of foreplay than exploring her mind.

Christy was having similar thoughts as she poured their coffee and led Adam into the living room. Like him, she was so aroused that even her skin tingled, but she wasn't ready to fall into bed. Her elation at seeing Adam standing on her doorstep hadn't overridden her observation skills. She had noticed the stress in his expression and the tense set of his shoulders. She'd also felt his anxiety when he'd kissed her, and she knew that whatever had upset him had brought him here.

Though it pleased her that he'd turn to her for comfort, she suspected that he was searching for physical solace when what he really needed was emotional support. Hopefully, she'd be able to provide him with both.

Adam was just as stunned by Christy's festive living room as he'd been the first time he'd seen it. Instead of joining her on the sofa, he began to wander around the room in tentative exploration. Initially he noticed the cute decorations, but he soon became aware of the religious ones, as well. She had to have a good two dozen Nativity scenes, and each was exquisite in its own way.

"You have a lot of Nativity scenes," he commented, more out of a need to break the silence than anything else. He was fascinated with the room, but he was also uncomfortable in it. He needed to hear the reassuring sound of her voice.

"I collect them," Christy explained.

He glanced at her thoughtfully. "You really like Christmas, don't you?"

"I was born on Christmas Day and my name is Christmas. I think it comes with the territory."

"I've heard that kids who have birthdays around the holidays feel cheated because they don't get as many presents as they would if their birthday was at another time of the year. Did you ever feel that way?"

"I might have if I'd had brothers and sisters," Christy replied, "but I was my parents' 'miracle baby,' and believe me, they never shortchanged me on presents."

"Why were you their miracle baby?"

"Mom and Pop tried to have a family for years, but for some reason Mom didn't conceive. Then, when she was forty-three and Pop was forty-five, I showed up. When I was born on Christmas Day, they declared I was a miracle, though I'd be willing to bet that they would have reached the same conclusion if I'd been born in the middle of July. When's your birthday?"

Adam smiled ruefully. "April fifteenth."

"Tax day!" Christy exclaimed incredulously. "Talk about a miserable time of year to have a birthday. Everybody's broke on tax day. You must have really looked forward to Christmas so you could get some good loot."

The change in Adam's expression was so instantaneous and so full of pain that Christy thought he'd become ill. She bounded off the sofa, but when she reached him and looked into his eyes, she knew his pain wasn't physical. "Adam, what's wrong?"

"Nothing, Christy," he assured gruffly as he noted her worried look. He brushed his hand over her hair, marveling at its silken texture. She was as beautiful and fragile looking as a treetop angel, yet it was an optical illusion. She was strong in both body and spirit, and he envied her that latter strength.

"You don't look as if you've been hit by a truck over nothing. Talk to me, Adam. Tell me what's wrong."

Adam stuffed his hand into his pants pocket and jingled his change, trying to decide what to say to her without sounding callow. He was thirty-seven years old, for pity's sake, and a mature man didn't become maudlin over his childhood. And if he was honest with himself, his childhood hadn't been that bad. Money had been tight, but he'd had a roof over his head, clothes on his back and food in his mouth. He'd also known that his parents loved him. It was only the holidays that had brought out the bitterness.

"Come sit down," Christy said determinedly as she urged him to the sofa. When he was sitting, she plopped onto the sofa sideways so she could face him. "Okay, Adam, talk."

"Christy, I told you that it's nothing."

"I said something that hurt you, Adam, and I want to know what it is."

He gave an exasperated shake of his head. "It's so silly that it would bore you. Let's talk about something else."

"No. I want to talk about this." When he shot her a look of reproach, she warned, "Dirty looks won't help."

"That wasn't a dirty look. It was an irritated look."

"Well, that won't help, either. You're going to tell me what's wrong if we have to sit here all night."

"Are you always this stubborn?"

"Yes. And you'd better get used to it. It's a family trait that's been passed down through hundreds—maybe even thousands—of generations, and I have it fine-honed to an art."

For some reason, her statement amused him. "You're something else, do you know that?"

"Uh-hmm, but changing the subject won't get you out of this."

The stubborn gleam in her eye assured Adam that she was speaking the truth, and that he needed to tell her about his childhood. Maybe if he talked about it, it would give him an idea how to start building a comfortable relationship with his father.

"All right, I'll tell you. But if you so much as smirk at how childish I'm being, I'm leaving. I do have my pride, you know."

Christy suspected that he had too much pride for his own good. "I won't smirk," she promised.

Adam leaned his head back against the sofa and stared at the ceiling. "I think I told you that my father was a construction worker. When I was five, he was laid off from work, which wasn't unusual, but this time it was just before Christmas. He took me aside and told me that he couldn't afford to buy me any presents, and I told him that it was okay, because Santa Claus would bring me presents."

He closed his eyes and gave a weary shake of his head. "You should have seen his face. He was only twenty-eight, but at that moment he looked a hundred and twenty-eight."

"And what happened then?" Christy prodded softly when he fell silent.

"He told me that there wasn't a Santa Claus, and that I had to be a big boy and accept that. When my mother found out what he'd done, she went through the roof and threw him out. Not long after that they were divorced, and I blamed myself. I just knew that if I hadn't mentioned Santa Claus, my dad would still be at home."

"It wasn't your fault," Christy said, blinking back tears. It tore at her heart to imagine how confused and frightened he must have been. Now she understood why he'd been so upset about having his picture taken with Santa Claus. It had to have revived that awful memory.

He turned to look at her. "I know that now. But for a long time I didn't, and after that, every Christmas got worse. Whenever December rolled around, my mother would start railing that she couldn't afford to give me a nice Christmas because Dad's child support was such a pittance. Then, after Dad remarried, my stepmother would complain that they couldn't afford a nice Christmas because child-support payments had them on the brink of bankruptcy. It got to the point that I cringed every time I saw a present under the tree with my name on it."

"How could your father let them do that to you?" Christy asked, incensed that two grown women had been so cruel, and one of them, his own mother!

Adam laughed, but the sound was mirthless. "He didn't let them, Christy. I doubt he even knew what was happening, because both of them had him in such a dither during the holidays that he worked two and sometimes three jobs in an effort to pacify them. But he was caught in a no-win situation, because then my mother would accuse him of not spending enough of the extra on me, and my stepmother would accuse him of giving me more than my fair share."

Christy's heart broke for the little boy who'd been caught in the middle. She reached for his hand and said, "I hope you won't take offense at this, but I don't think I'd like your mother or your stepmother. What they did to you is too cruel."

"Oh, Christy, don't judge them so harshly," he said as he laced his fingers with hers and brought her hand to his lips, pressing a kiss against her knuckles. "My mother was seventeen when she married, and twenty-three when she divorced. She was just a kid stuck with the responsibility of raising a kid. She had to be terrified at first, and when Christmas rolled around it was a reminder of why she was alone, so she struck out at my father. As the years passed, I think it became more a habit than anything else. I guess you could say that she'd fallen into a rut."

He paused for a moment, then continued, "As far as Marsha goes, she's ten years younger than my father, so she was only twenty when they married. She was another kid, and I think at first she was jealous of me. Later, she wanted to have a baby, but my father told her they had to wait until they had some money saved. Can you imagine how it must have grated to watch him write out that child-support check every month instead of putting it in the savings account toward their own family? It was only natural for her to resent me."

Christy couldn't believe he was defending them. "Don't make excuses for what they did to you. They were wrong."

"I'm not making excuses, and they were wrong," he agreed. "But in all honesty, it was only the holidays that were awful. The rest of the year, they were good to me."

Christy had her doubts about that, but thought it wise to keep silent. Good or bad, they were talking about his family. Instead she asked, "Why did you think this story was silly and childish? There's nothing silly or childish about it."

"Sure, there is," Adam argued with a self-deprecating smile. "I'm thirty-seven years old. I shouldn't let the past get to me, but every year it does. Which is ridiculous, since I haven't even celebrated Christmas for eighteen years."

Christy was so dumbfounded by his announcement that she was struck mute. When she finally found her voice, she said, "You haven't celebrated Christmas in eighteen years? Not even once?"

"Not even once."

"But you would have only been nineteen years old, eighteen years ago!"

He chuckled. "You're pretty good at arithmetic, and don't look so astonished, Christy. After I went away to college, my mother remarried and moved to Maine, so there was no reason for me to come home for the holidays."

"But what about your father? Didn't he want you to come home?"

"He asked, but I knew it was only an obligatory invitation, and even though I was on scholarship, I still worked part-time. Scholarships don't provide essentials like toothpaste and shaving cream. And by covering for kids who wanted to go home for the holidays, I made a killing."

"But what about after you graduated? Surely at some point you either came home, your family visited you, or you celebrated with friends?"

Adam shook his head. "Honey, as I've just explained, Christmas wasn't much fun in my family. Me coming home or them visiting me at that time of year would have had shades of *The Twilight Zone* written all over it. As far as my friends go, most of them are married and have kids. I would have felt as if I were intruding, so I always graciously declined their offers."

Christy was even more dumbfounded. To her, Christmas was the most special time of the year, and she couldn't imagine spending it alone. She'd find someone to celebrate with, even if she had to drag a stranger in off the street. To think that Adam had spent the holiday sitting at home by himself all these years was simply mind-boggling to her. But, then again, Adam being Adam, he wouldn't have been sitting at home. He'd probably have spent the day in his office shuffling through paperwork.

No wonder he didn't have laugh lines, she reflected as her gaze roved over his handsome face. And no wonder he was so reserved and withdrawn. He'd grown up in a world where the people he loved pulled away from him during the very season that was supposed to bring loved ones closer together. It was the most heart-wrenching story she'd heard in years.

"What's going through that delightful mind of yours?" Adam asked as he watched a kaleidoscope of emotions tumble through her blue eyes.

"That if you don't kiss me in the next five seconds, my lips are going to shrivel up," she answered.

"Now, we couldn't let that happen," Adam murmured as he brought his lips to hers.

She kissed him with a hungry urgency that swept away the last of his depression and made his heart soar. She was everything a man could want in a woman, and she'd be his at least through the holidays. It looked as if his secret wish of having one happy Christmas might finally come true.

"Christy, don't," he whispered hoarsely when her hand swept down his body and curved possessively around the bulge of his penis, making him so hard he was sure his zipper was going to be imprinted on the length of his shaft.

"Don't you want to make love with me?" she whispered back just as hoarsely as he slid his hand between her thighs and rubbed against the crown of her womanhood, creating a friction that had her instantly hot and wet.

"You know I do, but—"

"But what?" she encouraged as she continued to caress him wantonly.

He tumbled her onto the sofa and came over her. "I should be at the office."

"Then, by all means, I think you should go," she told him as she slid his sweater up his chest and pressed a kiss to one hard nipple peeking out from a crisp whorl of brown hair. Adam groaned, and thus encouraged, she flicked her tongue against it. He groaned again and reached for the zipper of her denims.

As he stripped off her clothes and started removing his own, Adam kept telling himself that they should move their lovemaking to the bedroom. But he needed to take her in this room that was the essence of her spirit. Last night he'd made love to Christy Knight, but tonight he needed to make love to Christmas Knight.

He was so aroused by the time they joined that he had to force himself to hold back, but the effort was worth it. Her skin reflected the multiple hues emanating from the Christmas-tree lights, and the colors shimmered and shifted with every passionate move of her body. He felt as if he were holding a living, breathing rainbow in his hands.

And he was in love with her. "I love you," he whispered so quietly that the words that came were no more than a silent breath of air. Then he kissed her as he made the one final stroke that pushed them both over the edge.

9

ADAM, FEELING GUILTY about spending two entire evenings away from the mall, vowed he wouldn't resurface until he'd attended to every single piece of paper in his In-Box.

When the intercom buzzed on his desk, he impatiently hit the button. "What is it, Vivian?"

"Christy Knight is here and would like to see you."

"Send her in."

He stretched while he waited for Christy, his impatience suddenly flaring into anticipation. He gave a wry shake of his head. He'd left her bed early this morning, but it felt as if he'd been away from her for years. How could he have fallen for her so hard in such a short time?

"Hi, boss," Christy greeted as she strolled into the room and closed the door behind her. Her gaze swept over his paper-strewn desk. "Busy day?"

"Yes," he answered, while studying her thoughtfully and trying to put together the impish-looking elf standing in front of him and the passionate lover he'd held in his arms for the past two nights. She was a complex composite of identities. Yet, he'd never known a more uncomplicated woman—Christy led with her heart. He felt both honored and humbled that she'd chosen to include him in her life.

"You're feeling guilty about all the time you've taken off for the past two days, aren't you?" she guessed as she settled into the chair in front of him and lifted her feet to the top of his desk.

"I am," he admitted with a rueful smile.

"I've really messed up your schedule, haven't I?"

"I don't remember complaining."

He tapped the end of his pen against his lips as he recalled how she looked with her hair spread over her pillow and her eyes darkening with desire. His body automatically stirred at the sensual memory of the silken feel of her skin sliding against him, and the soft purring sounds she made when she was aroused.

"Why are you looking at me like that?" she asked with a coquettish smile.

"You know exactly why." He leaned forward and propped his forearms on his desk. "To what honor do I owe this visit?"

"It's my lunch hour. I thought I'd stop by and see if you wanted to join me."

"I'd really like to, Christy, but I have to get some of this work done," he said as his gaze traveled from her green pointed shoes up the length of her legs.

"Have I got a run in my tights?" she asked when he frowned.

"No. I just realized how much of your legs is exposed. Don't you have some pants you can wear with that outfit?"

Christy would have sworn there was a tinge of possessiveness in his voice, but that was ridiculous. She'd been wearing the costume from the first day she'd met him. "I'm an elf, Adam. Elves dress briefly."

"In the winter they should wear pants," he muttered.

She grinned. He did sound jealous! "Why this sudden concern over my attire?"

"I don't want you catching pneumonia."

Her grin widened. "Well, if I get chilled, I'll figure something out. Would you like me to pick you up some lunch?"

He shook his head, his eyes still staring at her legs. "I asked Vivian to pick up something for me."

"Okay," Christy said, dropping her feet to the floor and standing. "I'll see you later."

She didn't even make it halfway to the door before Adam scooped her up into his arms and carried her back to his chair. He sat down, cradling her on his lap, and caressed her thigh.

"Take some time at lunch to look for a pair of pants," he told her. "I can't stand the thought of men ogling you."

"Adam, this outfit is hardly femme-fatale material. I'm dressed as an elf, for pete's sake!"

"You're going to fight me on this, aren't you?" he asked, his jaw tightening ominously.

"Nope. I'm going to ignore you," she countered, giving him a disarming smile. "You haven't complained in all this time, so you have no right to complain now."

"I didn't complain before because I kept coming down to the North Pole to look at your legs," he confessed. "Now that I can see them whenever I want, I want them covered up."

"Sorry, but the costume remains as is." She tried to climb off his lap, but he held her in place.

"What's your hurry?"

"I'm hungry, and my lunch hour is flying by."

"I could ask Vivian to pick up something for both of us," he said suggestively as he slid his hand farther up her thigh.

She caught his fingers before they could stray into more intimate territory. "I don't want to interrupt your work."

He kissed her, then murmured, "Are you sure you won't stay for lunch?"

She was tempted, but she knew they wouldn't be having lunch at all if he gave her a few more kisses like the last one. It wasn't that she'd mind making love in his office. However, it was the middle of the day and Adam's office tended to be like Grand Central Station. That was definitely too bawdy for her taste and, she suspected, for his, too. If they let things get out of hand, they'd both regret it, and she didn't want to do anything that might jeopardize their budding relationship.

"I'll take a rain check," she murmured back as she wiped telltale lipstick from his lips with her index finger. "You need to get your work done."

Adam reluctantly set her on her feet. "What are you doing for dinner?"

"Actually, I have a roast simmering in my oven. Would you like to come for dinner? I'll be eating around eight."

"I'd like that."

"Good. I'll see you at eight."

When she was gone, Adam stared at the door in bemusement. He'd never been as enthralled with a woman in his life, yet he was realistic enough to acknowledge that his time with her would be short. It might be true that opposites attract, but he knew that they didn't blend. But Christy was his for now, and for once in his life, he was going to go for the gusto and worry about the consequences later.

BY THE TIME eight-thirty came and went without even a call from Adam, Christy forced herself to hold on to her temper. She also sat down and ate. When he still hadn't arrived by nine, she placed the remainder of the roast in the oven and set the temperature at Warm. Then she returned to her darkroom.

Her father was right, she told herself as she began to work. Adam was going to break her heart. They'd made fabulous love two nights in a row, and he'd already forgotten her. The most frustrating part of the situation was that Adam had warned her it would be like this, but deep inside she hadn't believed him.

She resisted the urge to throw something heavy at the wall and made herself look at the situation logically. She was out to reform Adam, but she couldn't expect miracles overnight. Fighting with him about his time at the office would only turn him off. He had spent one entire afternoon and two nights away from the mall, so she had made some headway. It would have been a lot easier to be satisfied with that achievement, however, if he'd simply called to say he'd been delayed.

Nearly an hour passed before her doorbell rang. At least Adam had a knack of arriving at a convenient moment. She'd just reached the stage in the developing process where she could leave the darkroom safely.

"So, I see you finally arrived," she stated coolly when she opened the door.

He gave her a wary smile as he entered. "I'm sorry, Christy, but I got tied up at the office."

"You could have called," she said, hating the peevish sound of her voice, but unable to stop it.

"I tried, but your line is out of order."

"Oh, come on, Adam. You can come up with a better one than that," she muttered disdainfully. "I've made three or four phone calls since I've been home."

"Then it's only incoming calls you're having problems with."

He grabbed her by the arm and marched her through the house to the kitchen. There, he grabbed the receiver off the wall telephone and called the operator. After explaining the problem and asking for a call-back, he stood against the kitchen counter, folding his arms over his chest as he waited.

After several minutes passed and the telephone still didn't ring, he gave her a smug look. "Satisfied?"

Christy felt an inch tall. He was a workaholic, not a liar, and in his place, she would have stormed out of the house for having been accused of being one.

"I'm sorry," she said contritely.

"Hey, it's no big deal," Adam responded as he came to her and gave her a hug. "Next time, I probably will have forgotten to call."

"Have you eaten?" she asked.

"No. I was hoping you'd take pity on me and let me steal a sandwich."

"I'll go one better than that. Everything's in the oven warming. I'm afraid, however, that I need to get back to work, so you're going to have to entertain yourself."

"I have a better idea. I'll fix a plate and join you."

"You want to sit in the darkroom?" she asked dubiously. "It's pretty boring, Adam, and once you're in there, you'll have to stay for at least an hour."

"As long as I have something to satisfy my grumbling stomach, I'll be content to sit for as long as needed."

"Well, if you're sure, let's fix you a plate. So what held you up?" she questioned while they put his meal together.

"One of the businesses has a faulty alarm system. It kept going off, and it took me forever to track down the installer so he could come fix it. He was at a Christmas party."

"Mmm. Speaking of Christmas parties, I'm having my annual one two weeks from Saturday. Will you come?"

Adam automatically balked at her invitation. The only holiday parties he ever attended were the obligatory office parties. But before he could refuse, he looked over at Christy, who was watching him with eager anticipation.

"I wouldn't miss it," he told her, leaning over to drop a kiss on her lips.

"Great!" She sighed happily.

A few minutes later, they entered her darkroom, and Adam settled on her stool. As he ate, he surveyed the photographs she'd already developed.

"You do good work, Christy," he complimented. "Are you having trouble keeping up with the work load?"

"Not really," she answered. "Mom handles most of the tedious stuff. She packages the photographs and mails them for me. I guess you could say this job has become a family affair."

"What does your mother look like?" he inquired, curious.

She tilted her head, as if contemplating his question. "A lot like me, I guess, except she has gray hair and a few more wrinkles."

"You have wrinkles?" he teased, leaning toward her as if to look for them. "Where?"

"I always look my best in darkroom light," she replied with a laugh. "Eat your meal and be quiet."

"Does my talking bother you?"

His talking didn't bother her at all. It was his presence that was proving to be her undoing. The room was so small that every time he moved, her gaze was drawn to the play of muscles in his thighs. At this rate, it would take her two hours to get an hour's worth of work done.

"No, it doesn't bother me," she mumbled as she forced her attention back to her work.

Several minutes passed before he said, "Could you teach me how to do this?"

"You want to learn how to develop photographs?" she asked in surprise.

"Sure. I like to take pictures as much as the next guy, but I hate paying for the processing. There's something obscene about paying two or three times as much for the photographs as you pay for the film."

"Well, it would take a lot of processed film to make up the difference in the price of developing equipment and supplies. But if you're really interested, bring a roll of film with you some day and we'll go through the steps."

"Great. Who knows, I might learn a new profession, and a man should always be varied in his skills, right?"

Christy resisted the urge to tell him that as far as she was concerned, he was already varied in his skills quite nicely. "Right. I've reached a safe point, so if you'd like to go into the other room, now's the time to make a break for it."

"I'd rather stay here with you."

"You are a glutton for punishment, aren't you?"

"Yep." He set his plate aside, placed his hands on her shoulders and drew her between his legs. "Does this safe point allow for a welcome-home kiss? I didn't get one when I arrived."

"You were late, remember?" she remarked with a teasing grin.

"Only because your telephone was out of order."

She rubbed her hands against his chest. "Even if you had been able to get through, you still would have been late."

"Don't I get any credit for my efforts?" he asked huskily.

"Oh, yeah," Christy replied as he pressed his lips to hers and slid his hands down her spine in a seductive massage. "I still have a lot of photographs to develop," she reminded when he let her come up for air.

"One more kiss, and then I'll leave you alone," he promised.

Unfortunately, Christy knew that after one more kiss she wouldn't be able to leave him alone. She yearned to give in, but she had made a commitment to him and his mall, and to her clients. She wasn't about to let any of them down.

She smiled regretfully as she combed back the hair that had tumbled across his forehead. "I'm sorry, Adam, but the kiss will have to wait."

"Don't you trust me?" he asked.

"I trust you, but I don't trust myself," she answered. "Why don't you go watch television or something?"

"I have some work out in the car. Would I be committing the ultimate sin if I brought it in?"

"Not if you're willing to put it away when I'm finished in here."

"That sounds like a deal I can't refuse." He climbed off the stool and dropped a quick kiss to the tip of her nose. "One hour, and then I'll put my paperwork away."

She'd believe that when she saw it, but she let him think she took his word as gospel. As he walked to the door, she couldn't stop her gaze from sliding down him, which proved to be a definite mistake. "Adam?"

"Yes?" he said, turning toward her.

"I think I've changed my mind. Would you like to go back to the point where you asked me for another kiss?"

He reached her in two steps, and his answer seared her lips.

THE CROWD OF CHILDREN visiting Santa had slowed to a trickle. Christy changed the film in her camera and considered reaching for the Out To Lunch sign when her father yelped a frantic "Help!"

Christy spun around and widened her eyes in disbelief. One of the reindeer had managed to get his head through the "picture window" of Santa's living room and had his head resting on her father's shoulder.

"Dammit, Christy, he's trying to eat me alive!" Robert roared when the reindeer began to lick his face.

Christy couldn't help herself. She began to howl with laughter. Her father began to bellow a vitriolic string of curses, to which the reindeer responded with a few vitriolic bugles of his own.

The reindeer's owner rushed into the booth and tried to back the animal out of the window, but it grabbed a mouthful of her father's jacket and hung on for dear life. Christy joined in, but she was laughing so hysterically that she was more hindrance than help.

"What in hell is going on?" Adam yelled as he suddenly appeared.

He pushed Christy aside and began to unbutton Robert's jacket, but his efforts were hampered by Robert's flailing arms. To Christy, it looked like a scene out of a Keystone Kops movie, and she rushed to her camera and began to take pictures, though she was still laughing so hard, she wasn't sure they were even in focus. Finally, Adam managed to get her father's jacket unbuttoned, and Robert shot out of Santa's chair and rushed from the booth so fast, Christy was sure he'd broken a speed record.

"Are you all right?" she asked as she hurried after him. Her eyes were brimming with tears of mirth and she was practically choking, trying to hold back her giggles.

Robert scowled at her murderously as he folded his arms over his chest. "This is not funny, Christmas. That beast was trying to eat me!"

"Reindeer aren't carnivorous, Pop. He was just being friendly."

Her father opened his mouth to speak, but he was interrupted when Adam joined them.

"Are you all right, Robert?" he asked in concern as he began to help Christy's father back into his jacket.

"Of course I'm not all right," the older man snapped. "I was attacked by a vicious reindeer!"

"Oh, come on, Pop," Christy chided as she swallowed another burst of giggles. "He was licking you."

"He tried to bite me!"

"But he didn't," Christy soothed as she began to button the front of her father's jacket.

"I'm so sorry, Mr. Knight," the reindeer's owner stated apologetically when he joined them. "Are you all right?"

Robert opened his mouth, closed it, and then opened it again. Christy expected him to start railing at the man, but evidently the humor of the situation finally hit him. Her father began to chuckle. The chuckle deepened into a guffaw, and then he began laughing so hard that he clutched his sides and bent at the waist—at least, he bent as far as his pillow would allow. His laughter sent Christy into renewed gales of hilarity, until they were holding on to each other for support and gasping for breath.

"Care to give me the punch line?" Adam asked, unable to control the twitching of his lips as he watched them. He kept telling himself that the situation wasn't funny. When he'd arrived at the booth, it had been evident that Robert was terrified. The first thought that had sprung into Adam's mind was that the man might have another heart attack.

Christy glanced up at him and swiped at her eyes as another giggle escaped. "I guess you had to be there, Adam."

"Mm," he hummed noncommittally as he shifted his gaze to Robert. "Are you really all right, Robert?"

"I'm fine," Robert assured with a chuckle. He switched his attention to Christy. "I'm going home for lunch, and when I tell your mother how you laughed at me, she's going to—"

"Laugh her head off," Christy interrupted with a grin. She stood on tiptoe and pressed a kiss to his cheek. "I love you, Pop."

'Yeah, well, I love you, too," he responded gruffly.

Adam was captivated by the exchange. It was so natural, so easy, and he yearned to have the ability to express his innermost feelings so spontaneously. Several times during the past week he'd tried to tell Christy he loved her, but every time he found the words trembling on the tip of his tongue, he couldn't get them out.

"So, where are we going for lunch?" Christy asked Adam when her father left.

"How about my office?" he suggested with a leer.

The flagrant look of lust in his eyes made heat explode in Christy's middle and radiate south. "Gosh, you must be starving."

"Voracious," Adam agreed as he hooked his arm around her waist and drew her against him. He gave a shake of his head in self-reproach. "I'm not a teenager, so how come I feel like one whenever I'm around you?"

Christy wanted to tell him that it sounded suspiciously like love to her, but she wasn't sure he was ready to hear the words yet. Instead, she grinned and said, "Maybe you're just going through your second adolescence.

"Lord, I hope not," Adam muttered wryly and started walking toward the escalator. "I'm afraid my first adolescence wasn't that memorable."

"Oh, come on, Adam," Christy cajoled. "You can't fool me. You were a gorgeous hunk beating the girls off with a stick."

Adam shook his head. "Actually, I was a very shy teenager. All a girl had to do was smile at me and I practically had a nervous breakdown."

"You may have been a late bloomer, Adam, but on a scale of one to ten, I'd rate you a perfect twenty-five across the board," she pronounced throatily as they reached the second floor.

Adam laughed. She always knew what to say to make him feel as high as a kite. Not that she needed words. All she had to do was look at him to send him soaring.

"Well, in just a moment I'll see if I can't rate at least a twenty-six in the kissing department," he promised.

But Adam's vow was not to be fulfilled. When they walked into Vivian's office, he exclaimed in surprise, "Dad! What are you doing here?"

"Christmas shopping," Charles answered as he rose to his feet and gestured toward a pile of packages on the sofa. "I thought maybe we could have lunch together."

"Lunch?" Adam repeated inanely as he raked his hand through his hair. As far as he knew, this was the first time his father had set foot in the mall. He'd invited him to the grand opening, of course, but his father had had to work on an out-of-town job that day.

"Lunch," Charles repeated with a chuckle. "Like go to a restaurant, order a meal and sit down and eat together."

"I'd love to have lunch with you," Adam told him, feeling bewildered by this unexpected visit, "but I'm afraid I've already made plans to have lunch with Christy. By the way, this is Christy." He gestured toward her. "Christy, my father, Charles Worth."

"It's very nice to meet you, Mr. Worth," Christy responded, extending her hand while eyeing Adam's father curiously. The resemblance between him and his son was so strong that if it hadn't been for the silver in his hair and the laugh lines around his mouth and eyes, they could have passed for twins. "Why don't you join us for lunch?"

"Please, call me Chuck, and I wouldn't want to intrude," he declared as he glanced at Adam.

Adam knew it was his cue, and he offered reluctantly, "You wouldn't be intruding, Dad."

"Then, by all means, let's go dine," Charles said jovially.

They chose a small Chinese restaurant in the mall that served a luncheon buffet. The owner pulled Adam aside to discuss a business problem, and Charles and Christy went through the line and settled into a comfortable, high-backed booth.

"How long have you and Adam been dating?" Charles inquired as he accepted the soy sauce Christy handed him.

Christy glanced at her watch. "Nine days, twenty-three hours and forty-six minutes. Not that I'm keeping count, of course."

Charles chuckled. "Of course. However, if the two of you have been seeing each other for nine days, twenty-three hours and forty-six minutes, it sounds as if things might be getting serious."

Christy gave a noncommittal shrug. "Let's just say it has great possibilities."

"What has great possibilities?" Adam asked as he slid in beside her.

"The sweet-and-sour shrimp," Christy lied blithely while skewering one on her fork and extending it toward him. "I'm thinking of putting it on the menu for our Christmas party. What do you think?"

"*Our* Christmas party?" Adam repeated. For the past week, Christy had been talking about her annual Christmas party, but this was the first time she'd indicated it was going to be a joint effort. He liked the sound of it. It firmly established them as a couple.

"Of course it's our party. Now, tell me what you think about the shrimp?"

"Delicious," Adam answered as he took the offered tidbit.

Christy winked at his father. "The man has great taste."

"That goes without saying," Charles agreed, winking back.

Adam frowned as he glanced between the two of them, sensing that something was going on that he wasn't privy to. He shifted nervously on his seat, wishing his father hadn't popped up out of the blue like this. It was difficult enough to communicate with him without having Christy for an audience.

"So, where's Marsha?" he inquired.

"Marsha's my wife," Charles told Christy. To Adam, he said, "She's helping Dani decorate the nursery. The way the two of them are acting, you'd think the baby was going to be here tomorrow instead of two months from now."

"I heard that you're going to be a grandfather," Christy remarked. "You must be thrilled."

Charles smiled. "Yes, I am. When Adam and Dani were growing up, I was so busy trying to make a living that I didn't have the chance to enjoy them like I should have. But I suppose that's why God created grandparents. It's a second chance to make up for all the times we should have been there and weren't."

Christy would have had to be deaf not to hear the underlying wistfulness in his voice, and she glanced toward Adam, wondering if he also heard it. One look at his bemused expression, however, persuaded her he hadn't. She wasn't surprised. It often took an objective observer to see the forest for the trees, particularly when a person had been as hurt as Adam had been as a child.

"So, Adam, when can you come for dinner again?" Charles asked.

Adam blinked at the question. "Uh, gosh, Dad, I'm not sure. Things are so damn hectic around here, and until I find a manager—"

"Ah! I'm glad you reminded me," Charles interrupted as he raised a hip and retrieved his wallet. He pulled out a business card and handed it to Adam. "I ran into this young woman when we were doing some renovations on a minimall in Pueblo. She's the factotum down there. You know, the person who gets stuck with all the dirty work that no one else wants to do.

"Anyway, I was bragging about my son, the mall owner, and happened to mention you were looking for a manager. She told me she'd give her right arm for a chance at the job and asked me to give you her card. She says she has a degree in business administration and has been working at malls since she was sixteen. Not that that's saying much," Charles added with a laugh. "She can't be more than twenty-five or twenty-six, which is still a kid as far as I'm concerned. But she's personable, and I think she might be what you're looking for."

"Thanks, Dad. I'll give her a call," Adam replied, experiencing a strange mixture of feelings at his father's words. Part of him was both surprised and proud that his father had been bragging about him. Another part, however, was dismayed at his father's description of the woman as "still a kid." She was about the same age as Christy. Was he hinting that he thought his son was robbing the cradle? Considering the age difference between his father and Marsha, he knew that his father had no room to talk. Yet, maybe he was trying to warn him not to make the same mistake.

He glanced covertly toward Christy. As if sensing his sudden attention, she stared back and gave him the most beatific smile he'd ever seen. It arrowed its way right into his heart, and he knew that whether or not his father approved, it didn't matter. He wanted to sweep her into his arms and tell her that he was madly in love with her.

He might have followed through on the impulse if his father hadn't announced, "Well, I should get going. I told Marsha I'd pick her up around one-thirty, and you know how she is if I'm late. It was really nice meeting you, Christy, and I hope we see each other again soon.

"It was nice meeting you, Chuck," Christy responded sincerely.

"Come to dinner soon, Adam, and feel free to bring Christy with you," Charles said when Adam rose with him and they shook hands. Then he lowered his voice. "Hang on to that plum, son. She's absolutely adorable."

"That she is," Adam agreed with a sense of relief. His father hadn't been intimating that Christy was too young for him.

When his father was gone, he slid back into the booth and asked nonchalantly, "Well, what do you think of my father?"

"That if you're as gorgeous as he is at his age, you'd better keep in shape, because you're going to have a horde of little old ladies chasing you around the block," Christy answered.

Adam chuckled. "My father's right. You are adorable."

"Adorable?" she echoed, rolling her eyes in disgust. "Babies, kittens and puppies are 'adorable,' Adam. I'm not a baby, a kitten or a puppy."

"No, but you're an elf, so that makes you adorable."

"Good heavens, I'm going to have to do something about this perverse image you have of me," she grumbled.

"Don't you dare. I like you just the way you are," Adam murmured as he caught her chin and raised her lips to his.

His kiss was gentle, but filled with the promise of passion, and Christy quivered in response. She wanted to wrap her arms around his neck and make the kiss go on forever. Unfortunately, the paging system squawked his name, destroying the moment.

"Sorry," he muttered ruefully as he released her. "Gotta run."

"Adam, please call that prospective manager soon," she told him with a resigned sigh as he slid out of the booth. "I love the sight of your backside, but it loses something in the translation when it's hurrying away."

"You've got a deal," he said, leaning over to kiss her once more. "See you this evening. Think of somewhere special you'd like to go for dinner."

Christy sighed again when he left, and she popped the last of the sweet-and-sour shrimp into her mouth, mulling over the unexpected meeting with Adam's father. After Adam's Christmas horror story, she'd thought he'd be a small, stoop-shouldered man with a browbeaten, world-weary expression. Instead, he'd turned out to be a handsome, older version of his son.

The realization that she'd created such a false illusion made her wonder if she had other misconceptions about Adam. It dawned on her that though she was madly in love with Adam and had been his lover for the past nine—no, make that ten—days, she knew nothing about his life outside the mall. Good heavens! She didn't even know where he lived!

Well, that was going to change. Tonight she was going to start learning everything there was to know about the man she had every intention of marrying.

10

"YOU WANT TO WHAT?" Adam asked as he stared at Christy in disbelief.

"I want to have dinner at your place," Christy replied as she dropped into the chair in front his desk while he stuffed papers into his briefcase. It was one of the inroads Christy had made into changing his workaholic habits. He brought home a stack of paperwork and worked in her kitchen while she developed photographs. When she closed the darkroom, he closed his briefcase.

"Why?" Adam inquired, baffled by her bizarre announcement.

"Because I want to see where you live," she explained.

Adam gave a confused shake of his head. "It's an apartment, Christy, and it looks like a million other apartments. Besides, my cupboards are empty. I eat all my meals out."

"So, we'll order pizza."

"The place is a mess. My housekeeper's on vacation."

Christy smiled. "As you're well aware, I'm not the white-glove-inspection type, myself. A mess won't bother me."

Adam tried to think of another reason for staying away from his apartment, but his mind went blank. He knew, however, that he needed to come up with something. A home was supposed to be a reflection of its occupant, and his apartment was so bland that even he found it dull. Christy would probably take one look at it, see what a bore he really was and tell him *sayonara*.

"Christy, I'd prefer to wait until my housekeeper comes back," he said, stalling for time. If he could get her to wait a week, he could pick up some pictures to hang on the wall and maybe some plants. That should add a little life to the place.

Christy gave an obstinate shake of her head. "I want to see your apartment tonight."

Adam's temper stirred at her stubbornness, but he curbed it before he could say something he'd regret. Besides, he wasn't angry with her; he was angry with himself. He should have seen this coming. They were lovers, for pity's sake, and it was only natural for her to want to see where he lived.

"All right, Christy," he acquiesced with a sigh. "But don't expect much."

CHRISTY DECIDED THAT the kindest description she could apply to Adam's apartment was that it had great possibilities. He had an adequate collection of overstuffed contemporary and oak furniture, but his walls were bare and there wasn't a knickknack in sight. She'd been in wholesale furniture warehouses that had more personality.

"What a nice apartment," she commented, although she was actually thinking how desolate the place looked. No wonder he was content to live at the mall. She wouldn't have been eager to hurry home to this, either.

"I told you not to expect much," Adam reminded as he surveyed her features, trying to figure out what she was thinking. Unfortunately she didn't give him one clue, and a knot of nervous tension formed in his stomach.

"Well, now that you've seen the place, how about if we go to dinner?"

"I'd rather order pizza," she said as she placed her arms around his neck and pulled his head down for a kiss. "That way we can get down to some serious smooching."

Adam's stomach clenched with a new kind of tension as she molded her body to his and kissed him deeply, passionately. With a groan, he grasped her denim-clad bottom and lifted her. She wrapped her legs around his waist and rubbed her pelvis against his erection.

"We ... need ... to ... order ... the ... pizza," he told her, punctuating each word with an ardent kiss.

"Let's ... have ... an ... appetizer ... first," she returned, with ardent kisses of her own.

Adam didn't need any further encouragement and he carried her into his bedroom. They disrobed each other with the skilled frenzy of familiar lovers and collapsed on the bed, coming together quickly and eagerly. When their passion was sated, they cuddled, nuzzling and stroking each other.

"It's never been like this for me," Adam murmured as he smoothed Christy's hair away from her brow and gave her a tender smile. "You make me feel so alive."

"I know what you mean," Christy replied as she rubbed her hand against his jaw, enjoying the rasp of his five o'clock shadow against her palm.

"What do you think it means?" Adam asked pensively.

Christy caught her lower lip between her teeth as she searched his eyes. Did he really want an answer to that question? Maybe he didn't, but she needed to say the words. She needed him to know how she felt about him.

"Perhaps we're in love," she suggested quietly.

Adam closed his eyes as her words thrummed through him. As far as he was concerned, there was no "perhaps" about it, but he couldn't believe that she shared his love. It had to be an aberration that would end the moment the holiday season was over and she was no longer working at the mall. After all, out of sight, out of mind.

"Say something, Adam," Christy urged when he didn't respond.

"I don't know what to say," he answered as he opened his eyes and stared at her perplexedly. "It's happening so fast, Christy, and quite frankly, I can't figure out what you see in me."

"That's easy," she said as she ran her hand down his arm and caught his hand, lacing their fingers. "I see a strong, capable, hardworking man, who decides what he wants and goes after it with dedication and commitment."

"He sounds pretty stodgy to me," Adam observed wryly.

Christy shook her head. "You aren't stodgy, Adam. A bit too reserved at times, but never stodgy."

"You say that now, but will you still feel that way six months from now?"

"I suppose we'll have to wait six months and see," she replied, sensing it was time to lighten the conversation. Assuring him she'd still feel that way a hundred years from now wouldn't carry as much weight as showing him. "Why don't you order a pizza? I seem to have worked up a hefty appetite."

"Are you sure you wouldn't prefer another appetizer?" Adam murmured as he rolled to his back and pulled her on top of him.

"I might be tempted to indulge in another appetizer," Christy whispered breathlessly as his hands began to knead her breasts and his penis grew hard between her legs.

"I do love you, Adam," she gasped as he surged into her and sent her rushing toward climax.

Adam's tongue twitched with the need to return her vow, but he couldn't get the words out. Instead, he turned over, pulling her beneath him so he could show her with his body what he was incapable of expressing verbally.

WHILE ADAM CALLED the pizza parlor, Christy sat up in bed and stretched languidly. Then she scrutinized his bedroom. It had a bit more personality than his living room, because it at least had a lived-in look. His closet doors were open, giving an intimate display of his wardrobe. There were a couple of ties tossed on top of his bureau, and there was a book on the bedside table. Curious, she reached for the book. It was, of all things, a well-thumbed catalog of model trains.

"You like model trains?" she asked when he hung up.

"I like trains, period," Adam answered. He sat up against the headboard and pulled her back against his chest. "When I was twelve years old, I wanted to be a railroad engineer. I used to read everything I could get my hands on about trains, and I used to haunt a model-train store that was a few blocks from my mother's apartment. They had this fantastic American Flyer that I wanted so badly I could taste it. Unfortunately it was already a collector's item, and it cost a fortune. Here, let me show you a picture of it."

He flipped quickly through the pages until he found what he was looking for. "She's a beauty, isn't she?"

"Yes," Christy agreed, when in truth she couldn't see much difference between it and the other trains she'd been looking at.

He rested his chin on the top of her head. "Lord, I wanted that train. My parents couldn't afford it, so for months, I saved every penny I could get my hands on so I could buy it. But before I could come up with even half the price, it was Christmastime and someone else bought it. I was so upset that I never went back to the store. Did you ever want something so badly when you were a kid that you were absolutely crushed if you couldn't have it?"

"As a matter of fact, I did," Christy replied. "When I was ten, I wanted a skateboard. Pop was sure that I'd fall off it and break my neck, and Mom was certain I'd zoom out into traffic and get myself killed. For two years I begged them to buy me one, but they wouldn't give in. It was the first time they'd ever denied me something I really wanted, and I was sure that they didn't love me anymore."

"You apparently got over the trauma," Adam noted.

"Yeah. I turned thirteen and discovered boys and makeup. Pop decided he should have given me the skateboard and let me break my neck," she stated drolly.

Adam laughed and hugged her close. Then he said, "By the way, you've never said how your father feels about us seeing each other. He isn't upset about it, is he?"

Christy shrugged as she closed the catalog and laid it aside. "He's expressed a few reservations, but he's accepted us as a couple."

"You're sure? What you have with your father is very special, Christy. I'd hate myself if I thought I was causing problems between you."

"You're not causing any problems," she assured him, wondering if she dared probe into Adam's relationship with his father since he'd provided her with such a perfect opening.

Before she could make up her mind, the doorbell rang and Adam slid out of bed and into his slacks, explaining, "There's the pizza."

After he left the room, Christy reopened the catalog and looked at his coveted American Flyer. He'd admitted to being crushed when someone else had bought it, but it must have hurt him twice as badly to have lost it at Christmas. It had been just one more black mark against the holiday season.

Christy knew that she had to renew his faith in the spirit of Christmas. But how could she reach him in one season when he had so many miserable holidays to compare it with? It sounded like an impossible mission, but she knew she had to find a way to accomplish it. She loved everything about the holidays—from the mistletoe to the treetop angel. She couldn't bear the thought of Adam not being able to share that love.

CURSING, ADAM PACED his apartment and glanced at his watch for what seemed like the millionth time. Christy was supposed to have arrived an hour before. He threw open the sliding-glass door and stepped out onto his balcony, reconfirming what he'd already reconfirmed a half-dozen times during the past hour. Snow was piling up at an alarming rate and the wind velocity was near gale force. Had she been in an accident? Was she caught in a snowdrift somewhere? Should he call her parents? The hospital? The police?

He shivered violently, though it wasn't as much from the cold as it was from the images of doom and disaster his mind conjured up. Cursing again, he ineffectually kicked the icicle-encrusted wrought-iron railing.

When Christy had told him at lunch that she had an errand to run and would meet him at his apartment at eight this evening, he'd objected. It had already been snowing and the weather prediction was for blizzard conditions by late evening. But Christy had waved aside his protests, assuring him that she'd be fine. When he'd insisted that she let him go with her, she'd adamantly refused, telling him that this was an errand she had to do by herself.

Why had he let her persuade him to meet him here instead of letting him accompany her on her mysterious errand? Why had he let her go on the damned errand in the first place?

Because he'd have a better chance of bodily lifting a full-grown elephant than getting Christy to change her mind. She was the most stubborn woman he'd ever met in his life, and he loved her to distraction. If anything happened to her... He wouldn't let himself finish the thought.

He went back into his apartment and resumed pacing. He'd give her another half hour. If she wasn't here by then, he'd call the police, and if she was here by then, he'd shake her until her teeth rattled for scaring him like this.

Fifteen minutes later, his doorbell rang, and he rushed to the door and threw it open, ready to bellow at Christy, but his jaw dropped instead. She was panting from exertion and holding a huge evergreen tree that looked as if it were about to topple over on her.

"Merry Christmas!" she greeted cheerfully. "Give me a hand with this tree."

He jumped to her aid when the tree tipped precariously toward her. When he had a firm grip on it, he asked, "What am I supposed to do with it?"

"Carry it inside," she answered. "We're going to put up your very own Christmas tree tonight."

He parted the boughs in front of his face and peered through them at her. "I don't want a Christmas tree."

"Don't be ridiculous," she scoffed. "Everyone wants a tree." She strode into his apartment, stood in the center of the floor and tapped her finger against her lips as she studied her surroundings. "The corner by the sliding-glass door is a good spot. That way it can be seen from the street, but will still dress up the whole room."

"Christy, I don't want a tree," Adam repeated in slow, measured tones as he propped the evergreen against the wall. "In the first place, I'm not home enough to appreciate it, and in the second place, I don't celebrate Christmas, remember?"

"In the first place," she mimicked, "if you get five minutes of enjoyment out of the tree, then it has fulfilled its purpose. And in the second place, you don't celebrate Christmas because you have so many miserable memories of past holidays, but this year is going to be different, Adam. This year you're going to share Christmas with me, and I promise that you are going to have a glorious time. Now, put the tree over by the door. I have to run out to the car and get the decorations."

She was gone before he could object, and Adam eyed the tree warily. He had a premonition that if he put it up, something terrible was going to happen, but then he realized how foolish that sounded. It was simply a tree that you covered with tinsel, colorful balls and miniature lights. It had no mystical powers. It could cause him no harm, and Christy wanted him to have it, which meant he was going to have it whether he wanted it or not. With a resigned sigh, he carried the tree to the sliding-glass door just as Christy returned with three huge shopping bags.

"In these bags is everything a man needs to create the most beautiful Christmas tree in the entire world," she told him as she tugged off her coat and plopped down on the floor beside the bags.

Adam chuckled and shook his head, knowing that no tree could ever rival the beauty of her face lit with excitement. He knelt down beside her, watching as she pulled out box after box of garlands, tinsel, ornaments, lights, and finally, a cherubic treetop angel from two of the bags.

"Don't tell me you forgot to get a tree stand," he remarked when she looked up at him with a satisfied grin.

"Nope. It's in the last bag, but there's also a special surprise in there, so you have to close your eyes while I get the stand out."

He obediently closed his eyes and waited until she told him he could open them. Once they had the tree firmly in the stand, she announced, "Now, we need some mood music."

She turned on his radio, twirling the dial until she found a station playing Christmas carols. Adam wasn't surprised by the clear, sweet quality of her voice when she began to sing along with the sentimental rendition of "Silent Night." She was, after all, the embodiment of the season.

When the carol was over, she rubbed her hands together enthusiastically. "Let's get this tree decorated!"

Her gaiety was contagious, and Adam laughed with her as they strung lights. He even sang along with her in his husky, off-key baritone as they draped garland and tinsel. They playfully argued over the placement of the ornaments—he insisting that they should be symmetrically positioned, while she claimed they should be hung wherever you felt like it. They compromised by agreeing that he'd decorate the side facing the apartment his way, and she'd decorate the side facing the street her way. When they were done, she refused to put on the treetop angel, saying, "That's your job, Adam. It is your tree."

One look at her face assured him she wouldn't budge, and he gave in and performed the honors. When the angel was in place, Christy plugged in the lights, and Adam couldn't speak as he gazed at it. It might not be the most beautiful tree in the entire world, but he had to admit that it was gorgeous. He couldn't look away from it, even when Christy moved to his side, wrapped her arm around his waist and released a happy sigh.

"Merry Christmas, Adam," she murmured.

"Merry Christmas, Christy," he said huskily as he looked at her upturned face. His heart felt heavy with his love for her, and his body felt heavy with its need to express that love.

But before he could lower his lips to hers, she slipped out of his arms. "We aren't finished decorating yet."

She retrieved the bag she'd said contained a special surprise for him, sat down in front of the tree and patted the floor beside her. Adam sat in the designated spot as she pulled out a box and carefully removed a small Nativity scene, with miniature figurines anchored inside a wood-and-thatch stable.

"My grandmother gave this to me when I was five years old." She held it out to him. "I want you to have it."

"I couldn't possibly take it, Christy. You said it was a gift from your grandmother, so it has to have special meaning for you," Adam told her.

She gave him an angelic smile. "It's my most cherished possession, and that's exactly why I want you to have it. It's a token of faith, Adam. And regardless of what the future holds for us, I need to know that you have something tangible to reaffirm the meaning of the season."

Again she held it out to him. "I want you to take it and promise me that whether or not you celebrate Christmas in the years to come, you'll always take this out the day after Thanksgiving and put it where you can see it every day until the holidays are over." When he looked hesitant, she said, "Please, Adam. This is important to me."

Adam was so touched by her gesture that he felt the uncustomary sting of tears in his eyes. His voice was gruff with emotion when he took it from her and said, "If it means that much to you, I'll accept it, and I promise you that I'll always cherish it."

"And you'll always take it out the day after Thanksgiving and keep it out until the holidays are over, right?"

"Right," he agreed as he stood and placed it in the center of the dining-room table.

Then he returned to the tree, sat beside her again, and looked into her beloved face. "Tonight has been a night for new traditions. I've put up my first Christmas tree and received my first Nativity scene. So what other new traditions should we establish?"

Christy rose to her knees, wrapped her arms around his neck and rested her forehead against his. "I think we should christen the tree by making love."

He grinned devilishly. "I don't think the branches will hold us."

She laughed and pushed him to his back, straddling his hips. "*Under* the tree, silly."

"Oh," he murmured as he pulled her down to his chest and rolled so that her head was beneath the fragrant boughs. "Like this?"

"Like this." She sighed in satisfaction as he settled between her thighs and slid his hands beneath her sweater to cup her breasts. "Exactly like this."

CHRISTY WAS IN HER darkroom and Adam was working at her kitchen table when there was a knock at her back door. He scowled. It was nearly ten. Who would come calling at this hour of the night?

He opened the door and was startled to see a small, silver-haired woman standing on the porch with a suitcase at her feet.

"I'm Ilona Knight, Christy's mother. You must be Adam."

"Yes, I'm Adam, and let me help you with that," Adam said when she reached for the suitcase.

"That's very kind of you," Ilona replied as she entered the room and shed her coat. "I suppose Christy's working."

"Yes, but I'll go tell her you're here."

"Don't bother. This can wait until she takes a break." Ilona plopped into a chair at the kitchen table and sighed dramatically.

There was only one reason why Christy's mother would show up at this time of night with a suitcase, and he was trying to decide if he should go get Christy, when she walked into the room.

"Mom?" she said in surprise. "What are you doing here?"

"I've left your father," Ilona announced.

Christy laughed. "Sure, Mom."

"I'm serious, Christy. I've had it with him."

"What did Pop do this time?" she asked as she crossed to the stove and put on the teakettle. To Adam's surprise, Christy winked at him. He took the opportunity to point out the suitcase and was even more surprised when she grinned.

"What *hasn't* he done?" Ilona muttered in exasperation. "The man's a lunatic!"

"That's true," Christy agreed. "But he's a lovable lunatic."

"Ha!" Ilona exclaimed in disgust.

The kettle began to whistle and Christy fixed two mugs of tea. She carried them to the table, placed one in front of her mother, and then sat down. "So, what did Pop do?"

"He accused me of flirting with Mr. Wilson at the bank!"

"*Were* you flirting with Mr. Wilson?" Christy inquired as she took a sip of tea.

"Christmas Marie Knight! How could you even ask your mother a question like that?" Ilona responded indignantly.

"Because you do flirt," Christy answered.

"I do not flirt!"

"You'd better watch it, Mom, or your nose is going to grow."

Ilona folded her arms over her chest. "Okay, maybe I do flirt a little, but it's harmless flirting. The way your father acts, you'd think I was having an affair! If he doesn't trust me after forty-nine years, then there's no use going on with this marriage."

"I agree," Christy said solemnly, though Adam saw her lips twitch. "First thing tomorrow morning, I'll get the name of a sharpshooting attorney and you can take Pop to the cleaners."

"Good," Ilona responded with a satisfied nod. "Is it all right if I spend the night here?"

"Sure, but you know that this is the first place Pop will look for you."

"You just tell him that I'm not here."

"I won't lie to Pop," Christy declared. "If he comes looking for you, then you'll have to deal with him."

"But I never want to see him again!" Ilona wailed.

"Then I guess you'd better call a taxi and go to a motel."

"You know I hate motels."

"You either go to a motel, or you see Pop. You know as well as I do that he'll be pounding on the door within the hour, so you'd better make up your mind pretty quick."

"I guess I'll just have to see him," Ilona stated sullenly. "And I suppose I should tell him to his face that I'm filing for divorce."

"That would be the courteous thing to do," Christy said. "Why don't you have another cup of tea while Adam and I go upstairs and get the guest room ready?"

"I can prepare the guest room," Ilona offered, but Adam noted that she didn't make any effort to rise from the chair.

"No, I think you need to figure out exactly what you're going to say to Pop. We'll take care of the guest room." Christy rose to her feet and gave her mother's hand a reassuring pat. "Everything's going to be fine, Mom."

She gestured for Adam to follow, and he grabbed the suitcase and hurried after her. The moment they were out of earshot, he told her, "I think that under the circumstances, I'd better leave."

She grinned at him. "Don't be silly. Pop will be here any minute. They'll yell at each other for about five or ten minutes, and then they'll kiss and make up."

"I don't know about that," Adam said doubtfully. "Your mother is really upset. I think she's serious about filing for divorce."

"Believe me, Adam, she won't be filing for divorce, and she won't be spending the night."

"If that's true, then why are we making up the guest room?"

"We aren't." Christy caught his hand and led him into her bedroom. "We're going to stay out of the line of fire, and I'm sure we can find something interesting to do until they've worked things out."

"Dammit, Christy, how can you be so complacent about this?" Adam snapped when she took the suitcase away from him and wrapped her arms around his neck. "Your mother is discussing divorce!"

"Adam, Mom and Pop have a blowup like this once or twice a year. Mom's an inveterate flirt. Pop is a jealous fool. Despite what she says, she adores him for it. If she was seriously considering divorce, she wouldn't have come here where Pop would be sure to find her. She'd have gone to a motel."

"She said she hates motels," Adam pointed out as he unsnagged her arms from around his neck and began to pace. How could Christy be so cavalier about this? Her parents had been married for forty-nine years, for pity's sake. He'd heard Ilona Knight himself—the woman *was* serious about leaving her husband.

"Mom said that because it's her way of saving face," Christy replied.

"And what if it's not?" He stopped pacing, perched his hands on his hips and scowled at her. "What if your mother is serious? Do you know what it's going to be like for you to watch your parents break up just before the holidays? It's going to be hell for you, Christy. You're going to be miserable, and it's going to be my—"

"It's going to be your *what?*" Christy asked when he clamped his mouth shut and walked to the window. When he didn't respond, she went to him, wrapped her arms around his waist and rested her cheek against his back. "Talk to me, Adam. Don't shut me out."

"It's silly. It's childish. It's ludicrous," he muttered as he placed his hands over hers. "But even though I know that, I . . ."

"You what?" Christy prompted as she tugged on his shoulder until he turned to face her.

"If your parents break up, it will be my fault," he answered.

Christy would have burst into laughter at the absurdity of his statement if it hadn't been for the misery she saw in his eyes. He honestly believed what he was saying!

"How could it be your fault?" she inquired in bewilderment.

He raked his hand through his hair. "Because I'm a damn jinx when it comes to Christmas. I haven't celebrated it in eighteen years, and the first time I do, look what happens. Your parents are talking divorce after forty-nine years of marital bliss! It wasn't enough that I ruined my parents' holidays for years. Now I'm going to ruin yours, too!"

"You are right about one thing," Christy said, stunned by his words. She'd known he'd been terribly hurt as a child, but to realize that he believed himself bad luck was astonishing. "What you're saying is ludicrous. My parents' marriage hasn't been all bliss. They have their problems just like every other married couple, and if by some remote chance they do decide to divorce, it will be because they feel they can no longer make their marriage work. Don't try to endow yourself with godlike powers. *You* don't control their destiny. *They* do."

"But—" he began, but Christy cut him off.

"Adam, if this were any month but December, you wouldn't be blaming yourself. You'd be taking all of this in stride. But because it is December, you're expecting something bad to happen." She caught his face in her hands and made him look at her. "Nothing bad is going to happen, Adam, because I'm not going to let anything ruin your Christmas, and that's a promise I intend to keep."

"God, I love you," Adam whispered hoarsely as he slipped his arms around her and hugged her tightly.

It was the first time he'd said the words, and Christy's eyes filled with tears of happiness. "I love you, too," she whispered just as hoarsely when he lowered his head. Their lips touched, and she vowed that by the time the holidays were over, the hurt and scared little boy of Adam's childhood would be banished forever.

ADAM CHUCKLED AND SHOOK his head as he watched Robert and Ilona walk down Christy's drive arm in arm, stopping periodically to share a kiss. As Christy had predicted, her father had come pounding on the door, he and Ilona had screamed at each other for about ten minutes, and now they were behaving like lovebirds. Christy was standing in front of him, and he linked his arms around her waist and pulled her against him.

"That's what we're going to be like forty-nine years from now," Christy said as she rested her head against his chest.

As Adam gazed down at her silken head, he wanted that more than anything else in the world. He couldn't think of any better way to spend the remainder of his life than married to Christy, making a home with her and having a family.

"We won't be like your parents," he said, "because if you ever pack a bag and run away from home, I'll tan your hide."

Christy's heart performed a crazy little jig at his words. When she'd alluded to their future, it had slipped out unconsciously. The fact that Adam had responded so positively was more than she had hoped for at this stage in their relationship.

"You wouldn't lay a hand on me, and you know it," Christy countered as she turned in his arms and leaned against him, shivering in delight at the feel of his body pressed so intimately against hers.

"I wouldn't lay odds on it," he teased as he threaded his fingers through her hair.

She ran her tongue along the line of his jaw. "Well, the subject is moot, because I'd never run away from you. I'm a fighter, and a dirty one at that."

"Careful. You're giving all your secrets away," he said with a chuckle.

"No, just warning you. Let's go to bed. I'm suddenly very...sleepy."

"Then, by all means, we'd better get you tucked in."

He led her toward the stairs, and they climbed them, stopping every few steps to share a kiss. There was a new tenderness in their kisses—an underlying sweetness— that made Christy desire Adam more than she ever had before. She knew it was because he'd finally admitted his love. His avowal had strengthened the bonds growing between them, added a stability to their relationship.

Even their lovemaking took on new dimensions. They came together with an unhurried passion that was filled with gentle caresses and warm endearments, and when they finally reached the peak, their climaxes were long and far more satisfying. Christy knew at that moment that she'd never be able to love another man as much as she loved Adam. He was a part of her now, and her heart was his alone.

When he rolled to his side, bringing her with him, she tangled her legs with his, nestled her head in the crook of his arm and pressed a kiss to his chest in the area of his heart.

She was just starting to doze off when Adam said, "Christy, where were your parents' cars?"

"What?" she asked in confusion as she angled her head back so she could look at him.

"I just realized that I never saw your parents' cars. How did they get home?"

"Walked. They only live two doors down."

"They *what?*" Adam roared as he sat up in bed, sending her sprawling.

"Adam, turn off the light," Christy ordered impatiently when he switched on the bedside lamp. "You're blinding me."

Adam ignored her demand. "Your parents are your neighbors, and you didn't tell me? Do you know what that means?"

"That you didn't know that my parents were my neighbors," Christy answered.

"Dammit, Christy, stop being flip!" Adam railed.

"I'm not being flip," Christy argued. "And I don't know why you're so upset."

Adam gaped at her. "I'm upset because your parents know we're sleeping together. If I'd known they lived so close, I would have at least made an effort to be discreet!"

"You mean, sneak around," Christy said as she bolted up beside him, clutching the covers to her chest and glaring at him.

"I mean be *discreet*," Adam repeated angrily as he glared right back. "You may think it's all right to flaunt your sex life in front of your parents, but I think it's a damn affront."

Christy's own temper flared. "My parents aren't stupid, Adam, and I'm not going to insult their intelligence by pretending that our relationship isn't exactly what it is. I'm also not about to imply that all we have going for us is a tawdry backdoor affair. If you expect me to slink around and act as though I'm doing something shameful, then you have another thing coming!"

"But what about your parents?" he challenged.

"I'm sure they'd prefer that we weren't sleeping together without the benefit of a marriage license," she replied. "But they also know that I wouldn't be sleeping with you if I didn't love you. If they were really concerned, believe me, they'd confront me."

Adam cursed quietly and violently. In principle, he agreed with what Christy had said about slinking around as if they were doing something shameful, but he was still old-fashioned enough to believe that you didn't parade your love life in front of your parents. How in the world was he ever going to look either of the Knights in the eye again?

You could marry her. As enticing as the thought was, Adam knew it wasn't a viable solution, particularly after the confrontation they'd just had. It had shown a basic difference in beliefs and had all the shadings of a generation gap. How many other differences were there?"

"Adam, you're overreacting to this," Christy declared softly, placing her hand on his arm. "I love you, and I refuse to denigrate that love by treating it less than openly and honestly. I also refuse to accept your intimation that what we're doing is wrong."

"Oh, Christy," Adam responded with a heavy sigh, catching her face between his hands and tilting it up to his. "I'm not saying that what we're doing is wrong. But how would you feel if you were in your parents' place right now? Would you want to know what was going on? Would you want your neighbors to know?"

"Probably not," Christy conceded. "But I wouldn't want her sneaking around, either. It's far easier to deal with the truth than it is to live with suspicions."

Adam agreed with her in principle, but it didn't stop him from feeling like a jerk. If he'd known the Knights lived so nearby he'd never have—What? Never have made love with her? Maybe. But he doubted he'd have been that noble. However, he would have been more discreet.

But the damage was done, and he had two options. They could continue as they were, or he could end it here and now. He couldn't walk away from her—he was irrevocably in love with her. He could do nothing but pull her close and hug her so tightly his arms ached.

"If your father comes looking for me with a shotgun, it's going to be your fault," he told her gruffly.

She laughed. "Don't worry. My mother's no dummy. The moment she saw how jealous Pop was, she made him sell all his guns."

Adam caught her chin and raised her head. "Are there any more little revelations of this type that you've forgotten to tell me about?"

Christy shook her head.

"Good," he said as he lowered her back to the mattress. "I don't think my heart could handle any more surprises tonight."

"Really?" Christy whispered seductively as she trailed her hand down his flat abdomen and cupped him intimately. "Then I guess I'll just have to forgo the little surprise adventure I had in store for you."

Adam flashed her a wolfish grin. "I think you need a lesson in anatomy. My heart isn't even in that vicinity."

Christy released a delighted laugh. "I guess you'll just have to tutor me on the ins and outs of a man's body."

"Sounds good to me. Let's begin your lessons right now."

Christy agreed with a happy sigh.

11

"YOU LOOK ABSOLUTELY stunning," Adam said in awe when Christy paused at the top of the stairs.

It was the night of her annual Christmas party, and she was wearing a high-necked, long-sleeved gold velvet gown that would have been considered demure if it hadn't clung to her curves. Adam gulped as he watched her descend and the slit at the front of her narrow floor-length skirt displayed a tantalizing glimpse of leg with each step she took.

"I'm glad I meet with your approval," Christy murmured, pleased.

"Not only do you meet with my approval, but I can now fully sympathize with your father's jealousy of your mother. If you so much as smile at another man tonight, I'll probably deck him," Adam told her in a joking tone that was only half-feigned.

"I may share my smiles with other men, but my arms are reserved for you," Christy responded as she reached the next-to-the-bottom step. They were at eye level, and she wrapped her arms around his neck. "How about a kiss?"

"I might get you all wrinkled," Adam warned as he placed his hands on her waist. The feel of plush, soft velvet was so sensuous that he groaned as he ran his hands down her hips and cupped her bottom, bringing her up against him.

"I don't mind a few wrinkles," Christy mumbled as she touched her lips to his. She trembled as desire flicked through her. The doorbell rang, reasserting sanity. "I think the first of our guests have arrived."

"I'm not sure I'm in any condition to greet them," Adam noted tautly.

"You can use me as a shield," Christy offered impishly as she took his hand and led him toward her studio and the front door.

Within the hour, the house was packed and Adam had long ago lost sight of Christy. He also felt as if he'd been transported to the Land of Oz. It wasn't that Christy's friends weren't nice. It was that they were all so young. Except for Robert and Ilona, he was the only person in the room over the age of thirty, and as he wandered from group to group looking for Christy, he became more and more aware that he had nothing in common with these people.

When a twenty-minute search still hadn't turned up Christy, he fixed himself a stiff Scotch and water and retired to a corner of the studio to nurse it. Robert joined him a short time later.

"God, I hate that music," Robert muttered, plopping into the chair beside Adam's as Guns n' Roses blared from the CD player.

"I'll drink to that," Adam agreed, lifting his glass in a mock toast. "Whatever happened to good old rock and roll?"

"Rock and roll?" Robert repeated disparagingly. "Hell, whatever happened to real music where you can hold a woman in your arms? You can give me Glenn Miller any day."

"I suppose music is the most noticeable sign of a generation gap," Adam commented.

Robert chuckled. "It's usually the first one to hit you over the head."

Adam had to agree with that, because it had just hit him over the head. The point was brought home even harder as his eyes strayed over the crowd, and he had a sudden flashback of his father and Marsha in an argument when he was child. His father had been complaining about going to a party given by some of Marsha's friends. He'd told her that he felt like a duck out of water, because he didn't even know what they were talking about half the time.

At the moment, Adam could certainly empathize with his father. It wasn't that he didn't know what Christy's friends were talking about, it was simply that he had nothing to contribute. They had shared histories and shared friends, which, of course, dominated their conversations. Some of them were still in school, working toward master's degrees and Ph.D.'s in subject areas that hadn't even been heard of when he was in college. Others were engaged to be married, newly married, or had just become parents, so they were discussing crystal and china patterns, mortgage interest rates and diaper rash. Though all of them had been friendly and tried to include him in their conversations, he'd sensed that they were as ill at ease with him as he was with them.

Suddenly Christy materialized at the far corner of the room, and as Adam watched her engage in animated conversation with a group of her friends, he couldn't have felt further removed from her if an ocean had separated them. This was her world, and he simply didn't fit in.

Sadness enveloped him, accompanied by a pang of regret. He loved her to distraction; and because he did, he knew that he was going to have to let her go. He also knew that the sooner he did it, the better off they'd both be.

CHRISTY WAS EXHAUSTED by the time she ushered the last of her guests out the door. The minute she closed it, she collapsed against it and released a weary sigh.

"Tired?" Adam questioned solicitously as he walked up to her and brushed a lock of hair away from her cheek.

"Wiped out," Christy answered as she wrapped her arms around his waist and rested her head against his chest. "But it was a wonderful party, wasn't it?"

"It was very nice," Adam replied.

An uneasy shiver tracked its way down Christy's spine. It wasn't his words, but his tone of voice that alerted her to the fact that something was wrong. He sounded so . . . distant.

"What's wrong?" she asked as she pulled back so that she could see his expression.

"Nothing." He flashed her a smile, but she noted that it didn't reach his eyes.

"Don't lie to me, Adam. I know you too well."

She watched an uncustomary blush darken his cheeks. "We can talk about it tomorrow. You're exhausted and need to go to bed."

Another shiver made its way down her spine, but this one was of pure fear. If he'd sounded distant before, he now sounded light-years away. "I want to talk about it now."

"Christy, it can wait until tomorrow," Adam said with a frown.

"No. Something's wrong, Adam, and I want to know what it is."

"Why are you always so damn stubborn?" he muttered irritably as he stepped away from her and raked his hand through his hair.

"Because that's the only way I can ever get a straight answer out of you," she retorted with an angry toss of her head.

"I don't want to fight with you, Christy."

"Then tell me what's wrong."

Adam glared at her and she glared right back. Several seconds passed before he mumbled a curse and gave in. "All right, I'll tell you what's wrong. It's us. We don't belong together."

"I see," she said. "And just when did you come to this conclusion?"

"I've known it all along, but I've ignored it. I kept telling myself that we could work it out, but tonight I recognized we can't." She opened her mouth to speak, but Adam held up his hand. "You can argue with me until you're blue in the face, but it isn't going to change the fact that I'm too old for you."

"You're not going to start that again?" Christy questioned in disbelief.

"Yes. Because it's the truth and your party proved it. I have nothing in common with your friends. I couldn't even carry on a conversation with them. I felt like an alien from another planet. I don't belong in your world. Hell, I can't even stand the music you listen to!"

Christy allowed time for his complaints to sink in before she replied, "I can see where you may have felt uncomfortable tonight. You were in a roomful of strangers, so the next time we have a party, we'll invite your friends, too. We'll even mix the music so we accommodate both our tastes."

"It isn't that simple," Adam rebutted. "Can't you see that this is only one element of our life-styles that doesn't mesh? As time passes, we'll find more and more areas, and not all of them are going to be so easy to compromise."

He gripped her arms gently but urgently. "Christy, I love you, but I know what I'm talking about. My stepmother is ten years younger than my father. As a kid, I watched them struggle through their age differences. They fought constantly and bitterly. They're miserable, and I couldn't stand to see us end up like that."

"Adam, how long have your father and stepmother been married?" Christy questioned.

Adam gave her a puzzled look. "I was seven—so, close to thirty years."

"Thirty years," Christy repeated. "Do you honestly believe that they would stay married that long if they were so miserable?" Before he could respond, she said, "Adam, married people fight, especially newly married people. It comes with the territory. And you haven't lived around your family for years, so how do you know your father and stepmother are miserable? Have you asked them?"

"Of course not," he said impatiently.

"Well, I'd suggest that before you start measuring our relationship against theirs, you find out exactly what their life is like. Ask your father if he's miserable. Ask your stepmother if she's miserable. Ask them if they'd still get married if they had it to do over again. Once you have the answers, I'll be happy to discuss this subject with you in further detail. In the meantime, I'm going to bed. Are you coming?"

"Why don't you ever listen to me?" Adam asked as he dropped his arms to his sides and gave a resigned shake of his head.

She caught his face in her hands and stared deeply into his eyes. "I do listen to you, but what I'm hearing doesn't make any sense. Talk to your father," she urged. "Find out if what you perceive about his life is true. I have a feeling that you're in for a big surprise."

"And what if I'm right about them?" he challenged.

"Right or wrong, it won't change the way I feel about you. I love you, and I'm going to fight for you. Now, come to bed. As Scarlett O'Hara would say, we'll worry about it tomorrow."

"You are so maddening," Adam muttered.

Christy grinned. "I know. But that's one of the things you love most about me."

Adam didn't contradict her, because it was the truth.

"ADAM!" MARSHA SAID in surprise when she opened the front door.

"I'm sorry to drop in like this," Adam apologized, chiding himself for not calling first. He'd been on his way to the mall, and before he'd even realized what he was doing, he'd pulled up in front of his father's house. For a moment he'd considered driving away, but then he'd recalled what Christy had said last night. Was it possible that she was right? Did he have the wrong impression about his father's marriage? "If Dad's around, I'd like to see him. I won't stay long."

"Chuck is in the shower, but he shouldn't be much longer. And please don't apologize for dropping in. You're welcome any time," Marsha said graciously as she gestured him inside.

"Thanks," Adam replied as he followed her into the living room.

"Would you like some coffee?" Marsha asked.

"No, I'm fine." He sat on the edge of the sofa and nervously laced his fingers together. "How's Dani?"

"She's doing great, and I know she wants to see you. She was very disappointed that you missed Thanksgiving dinner."

"Yeah, well, I had a million things to do before the mall opened the next day. I'll give her a call. Maybe we can get together for lunch."

"I know she'd like that."

A strained silence fell between them, and Adam said, "You don't have to entertain me, Marsha. Please, go back to whatever you were doing."

"Actually, I was trying to build up enough courage to ask if we could talk before your father comes downstairs," Marsha replied.

"Talk?" Adam repeated warily.

She nodded and sat down on the edge of his father's recliner. "I owe you an apology, Adam. Until you went away to college and never came back, I didn't comprehend how mean I'd been to you while you were growing up."

"You weren't mean, Marsha," Adam stated.

"Oh, yes, I was," she countered with a brittle laugh. "Heavens, Cinderella had it better than you. I could come up with a million reasons why I treated you the way I did, but I'd only be trying to justify myself, and there isn't any justification for my behavior. All I can say is that I'm sorry, and ask you to give me another chance. If you can't do it for me, would you do it for your father? He wants to be close to you, Adam, and it's killing him that you're keeping him at arm's length."

"It's killing me, too," Adam whispered as he met her gaze head-on.

Marsha's eyes filled with tears, and she gave a sad shake of her head. "Then I'm even more sorry, and I'm glad we had this talk."

"Adam?" his father questioned in disbelief as he chose that moment to walk into the room. "What's wrong?"

"Nothing," Adam said as he surged to his feet. "I just wondered if we could talk. I, uh, sort of need some fatherly advice."

"Well, sure," Charles answered, his expression stunned.

"I'm on my way to the grocery story," Marsha announced as she rose hastily. "Why don't you two make yourselves at home in the kitchen? There're some blueberry muffins on the counter, and a fresh pot of coffee. I won't be home for a good hour. It was nice seeing you, Adam, and don't be such a stranger."

"I won't, Marsha, and thanks."

She nodded and left, and Charles said, "Let's go into the kitchen."

While Charles poured coffee and brought the plate of muffins to the table, Adam tried to figure out how he wanted to approach the subject of his father's marriage.

He was still struggling with the dilemma when Charles sat down at the table across from him and said, "So, what's on your mind?"

Adam cleared his throat uncomfortably. "It's Christy. As I'm sure you could tell when you met her, she's quite a bit younger than me. Twelve years, to be exact."

"And that bothers you?"

Adam shrugged. "Most of the time it doesn't, but she had a party last night, and I didn't fit in. I remembered you and Marsha fighting about the same thing once, and I wondered if . . ."

"If?" Charles encouraged when he didn't continue.

"If you've ever regretted marrying Marsha," Adam finished.

"Yes and no," Charles answered with a grin. "There isn't a married man—or woman, I'm sure—who hasn't regretted getting married at one time or another. But those phases usually pass quickly."

"Then, if you had it to do all over again, you'd still marry her?" Adam inquired.

"In an instant," Charles replied. "Marriage is never easy, Adam, and an age difference presents its own unique problems. But if two people really love each other, and they're both committed to doing everything they can to make their marriage work, then they have a pretty good chance of making it."

Chagrined, Adam stared down into his coffee cup. Christy *had* been right. His father's marriage wasn't as bad as he'd perceived it. As a child, it had been their arguments that had made the strongest impression, but as he thought about the past, he could also recall times when he'd seen his father and Marsha sneak kisses and hugs. He could remember them sharing soft, intimate laughter, holding hands, and dozens of other loving gestures.

The love had always been there, but he hadn't seen it, or maybe he hadn't wanted to see it, because then he would have had to accept that his parents' marriage was really over—that his father was never going to come home; that he and his mother and father would never be a family again.

"Have I helped?" Charles asked.

Adam glanced up and nodded. "You have, and thanks."

"Any time."

They rose from the table and Charles extended his hand. Adam took it, and then on impulse, he stepped forward and gave his father a hug. When Charles hugged him back, Adam knew that they were finally on the road to friendship, and he owed it all to Christy. Without her encouragement, he would have never come. It made him love her all the more.

CHRISTY WAS HAVING a similar meeting with her mother. Ilona was quiet as Christy told her about Adam's complaints after the party and his insistence that he was too old for her.

"It's ridiculous," Christy concluded. "But how do I convince him of that?"

Ilona settled at the table and said, "I think he has to convince himself, Christy."

"But if I sit around waiting for him to do that, he'll convince himself right out of our relationship!" Christy objected. "There has to be something I can do."

"Something you can do about what?" Robert demanded as he wandered into the kitchen with a sleepy yawn.

"About Adam," Christy muttered. "He thinks he's too old for me, and don't you dare agree with him!"

"I wouldn't dare," Robert mumbled as he gave Ilona a good-morning kiss before heading for the coffeepot. "I'm too pooped to put up with one of your tongue-lashings."

"Good. That means you can help me come up with a plan to show him he's wrong."

Robert glanced over his shoulder as he filled a mug. "*Moi?*"

"Yes, you," Christy replied disgruntledly. Then she frowned as she watched him retrieve a pack of cigarettes from the cupboard and extract one. "Why are you smoking? The doctor told you you weren't to smoke!"

"I have one cigarette a day, young lady. And if it puts me in my grave, so be it," he declared churlishly. "Now, tell me why Adam suddenly decided he was too old for you."

Christy knew he was changing the subject, and she scowled at the cigarette as he lit it. She considered lecturing him, but knew he wouldn't listen to her. He was more stubborn than she was.

"It was the party," she explained. "He claims he has nothing in common with my friends and he hates my music. I told him that the next time we'd invite his friends, too, and that we'd mix the music to accommodate both our tastes. But he says that this is only one element of our life-styles that doesn't mesh, and other areas won't be as easy to compromise on."

"Damn, the man's brighter than I thought he was," Robert stated genially.

Christy gave him a baleful look. "Pop, I swear that if you encourage him in this foolishness, I will never speak to you again. I love Adam. I want to marry him and have a dozen kids with him, and I'm going to find a way to do that if it kills me."

"I think, dear, that that would be defeating your purpose," Ilona noted with a chuckle.

"Why aren't the two of you taking this seriously?" Christy wailed.

"We are, Christy," her mother assured. "But you can't force Adam to see things your way."

"For once, I agree with your mother," Robert said. "Right now, your hormones are all stirred up and they make you feel invincible. Eventually, everything is going to get back on an even keel. When that happens, you're going to get slapped in the face with reality, and that's probably what happened to Adam last night. Instead of fighting him, why don't you sit down and make a list of problems you think might come up and possible solutions? Then sit down with him and discuss them. Maybe that will encourage him to do the same."

"You know, that isn't such a bad idea," Christy mused.

"Well, of course it isn't. I thought of it, didn't I?" Robert retorted.

"Yes, Pop, you did," Christy admitted with a grin. "And I almost love you for it."

He frowned at her. "What do you mean, *almost* love me for it?"

"I don't love people who smoke, even if it is only one cigarette a day," Christy quipped as she leaped to her feet and headed for the back door. "I'll see you two later. I need to talk to Adam before I go to work."

ADAM WAS ON THE PHONE when Christy stuck her head in his door. He smiled and gestured her inside, holding up two fingers, which she understood to mean he'd be on the line a few more minutes.

She resisted the urge to pace and forced herself to sit in the chair in front of his desk while she waited for him to conclude his business. Her instincts told her that if she was to persuade him that their love could withstand anything, including age, she had to appear cool, calm and collected.

When he hung up, he rubbed his hands together in anticipation. "I think I may have found a manager."

"Adam, that's great!" Christy exclaimed in excitement, momentarily forgetting her mission upon hearing the news. "Who is it?"

"That young woman my father told me about. I'm going to Pueblo tomorrow to interview her in person, but at this stage that's just a formality. I'm ninety-nine percent sure that she's right for the job."

"Yeah. Well, speaking of being ninety-nine percent sure, I've been thinking about what you said last night, and—"

"Yes, about last night," Adam interrupted as he rose from his chair and rounded his desk. "Before you go any further, you should know that I stopped by to see my father this morning."

"You did?" Christy asked, gazing up at him in shock. "Well, don't keep me in suspense. What did he say?"

"You were right," he said, grabbing her hand and pulling her up into his arms. "He's not miserable. And he swears that if he had it to do over, he'd still marry Marsha. While I was talking to him, I realized that there was always love there. I just didn't want to see it, because then I'd have to accept that he wouldn't be coming back to me and my mother."

"Oh, Adam, it breaks my heart when I think of how forlorn your childhood was."

"Don't cry," he whispered huskily as he watched tears well in her eyes. He pressed a kiss to each of them. "The past is gone, Christy. It's time I started concentrating on the present and the future."

Christy drew in a deep breath. "I agree, which is why I stopped by. Pop thinks we should make up a list of potential problems we see in our relationship so we can discuss them and come up with solutions. How does that sound to you?"

"Actually, it sounds too damn analytical, but it's probably a good idea. For now, though, let's just concentrate on being in love. We can worry about lists later."

The love glowing in his eyes as he stared down at her made Christy's heart swell to near bursting.

"Speaking of lists, what do you want for Christmas?" she asked.

Adam slid his hand down her spine, cupped her bottom and pulled her against him. "Santa's already given me exactly what I want. I love you."

"And I love you," she returned as she rose on tiptoe and pressed her lips to his, deciding that Santa had given her exactly what she wanted, too—well, almost exactly. The coup de grace would be a ring on her finger, and if she had her way, that would happen very, very soon.

FOR THE FIRST TIME in thirty-two years, Adam was eagerly looking forward to Christmas. Since it was Christy's day off, he spent his lunch hour wandering through the mall looking for the perfect gift for her. He was leaning toward a pair of sapphire earrings that matched her eyes, but he was drawn time and again to the engagement-ring display.

He kept telling himself that it was too early to even consider marriage. They'd been dating less than a month, and though Christy kept insisting she was in love with him, he couldn't help being wary. Their relationship seemed too good to be true, and the pessimistic part of his soul insisted that it was only a matter of time before it all went awry.

But Adam planned on doing everything in his power to keep that from happening. Yesterday he'd hired Lana Wilkens as his new manager, and she'd start work the day after New Year's. Christmas was still a week away, but the mall had already far exceeded his financial expecta-tions, and the crowds were growing larger instead of smaller. Of course, the true test of the mall's success would be after the holidays, and the odds were that a few businesses wouldn't survive. But he already had a wait-ing list of other businesses ready to move in. It was as if fate was finally riding on his side, and he was sure that it was because of Christy. She was not only the love of his life; she was his good-luck charm.

He bought the earrings and had them gift-wrapped. Then he headed back toward his office, but as he passed the toy store, a display of skateboards caught his eye. He stopped and stared at them for a long moment, recalling how badly Christy had wanted one as a child.

Though he told himself that it was a ridiculous gift to give a grown woman, he knew he had to get one for her. She might never use it, but he knew in his heart that the skateboard would mean more to her than a dozen pairs of expensive earrings. By the time Adam returned to his office, he was positive that nothing could ruin the holi-days this year. Absolutely nothing.

12

ON CHRISTMAS EVE morning, Adam woke Christy with teasing kisses, and she smiled up at him contentedly.

"What are you doing?" she murmured with a yawn.

"Waking you up so I can wish you a Merry Christmas Eve," he answered with a grin. Then he gave her bottom a playful pinch. "Besides, it's time for me to get up so I can go home and change."

Christy wound her arms around his neck. "Adam, as soon as the holidays are over, we need to make some decisions."

"What kind of decisions?" he asked warily.

Christy drew in a deep breath for courage. "Well, for one, I think we should live together so you're not always racing back to your apartment to get ready for work."

"Live together?" he repeated, frowning at her. He'd been looking at engagement rings, and she was talking about living together? "I don't believe in people living together."

"Well, we can't keep on like this," she told him as she sat up in bed. She clutched the sheet to her chest. "I'm not going to have you flying between our homes day after day. Either we start living together, or—"

"Or what?" Adam questioned sharply when her voice trailed off. If she thought she was going to blackmail him into living with her, then she had another thing coming. He didn't want to live with her. He wanted to marry her!

"Or we get married," she answered with a defiant tilt of her chin.

Adam released the breath that he'd been unconsciously holding. He took her in his arms and gave her a kiss. Maybe it wasn't too early, after all, to pick up an engagement ring.

"We'll talk about this tomorrow," he stated roughly, catching her lips in a steamy kiss that instantly drove the conversation from her mind. "Damn," he rasped as he sighted the alarm clock. "I don't have time to finish this."

"Well, Mr. Worth," she drawled as she slid her hands down his back to his firm buttocks and pressed him against her, "I'd suggest that in future you don't start what you don't have time to finish."

"Well, Ms. Knight," he drawled back, "in the near future, I'll have a manager, so I'll have plenty of time to finish what I've started. Are we having lunch together?"

"Unless you cancel out."

"What about dinner?"

"That, too. And we're going to do something special tonight, so let's meet at your apartment at seven."

He lowered her to the mattress and tugged away the sheet. Then he laved his tongue across one breast. "I think you need a sample of the something special we're going to do tonight," he mumbled as he moved to her other breast.

Christmas would have berated him for his seductive teasing that had her squirming beneath him, except that she could feel his own response and knew he was going to be suffering as much as she was.

"That isn't the kind of 'special' I had in mind," she gasped as he began to rain kisses from her sternum to her navel.

His kisses moved lower. "Are you saying that we aren't communicating on the same wavelength?"

"No, we're not. Adam!" She shuddered when his lips touched her intimately. "We don't have time for this, remember?"

"I'm making time," he whispered roughly. "It's Christmas Eve, and we need to start celebrating."

They celebrated, all right, and though the holidays had always been special to Christy, they had never been as joyful for her as they were this year. She was in love, and she knew that this holiday season was going to be the beginning of a new era for Adam. Never again would he have an unhappy Christmas, she vowed to herself as he brought her to fulfillment. Never.

"CAROLING!" Adam exclaimed that evening when Christy showed up at his apartment and announced that they were going Christmas caroling with a group of shop owners from the mall and their families. "Christy, I can't even carry a tune!"

"No one cares, Adam." She reached up to adjust the collar of his shirt. "This is for fun. We're going to a couple of nursing homes and the children's ward at the hospital. It's only for a few hours."

Adam looked toward the Christmas tree. He'd plugged in the lights, which flickered over a dozen gaily wrapped packages, most of them for Christy. He had champagne cooling in a bucket of ice, and his own special spaghetti sauce bubbling on the stove.

"I made special plans for us," he grumbled.

She tugged on his collar until he lowered his head so she could press a kiss to his lips. "Two hours, Adam."

Adam still didn't want to go, but Christy was looking up at him with such expectancy, he capitulated. "All right. Two hours, and then we come home. I didn't spend the afternoon cooking spaghetti sauce for nothing."

"You took the afternoon off?" Christy asked in disbelief, and then laughed when he nodded. "I've made better progress with you than I'd thought."

"Well, you'll lose ground very fast if my sauce burns, so why don't you turn it off while I change?"

Christy did as he asked, nearly changing her mind about caroling when she saw the champagne chilling and realized that Adam had indeed made special plans. But she had to get him out of the house. She'd bought Adam an American Flyer train set, just like the one he'd wanted as a child. They'd had dinner with his family a few nights before, and she'd arranged for Adam's father to set up the train beneath the tree while she got Adam out of the house.

When Adam joined her, she regarded him with appreciation.

"Two hours," Adam reminded her gruffly as he watched her inspect him in such a wanton manner that he was instantly aroused.

"Two hours," Christy promised as she raised her gaze to his face. "Lord, that sounds like forever."

"We could stay home."

Christy shook her head. "Think how much better it will be after all that anticipation."

Adam retrieved his coat.

CHRISTY HAD HAD EVERY intention of adhering to her two-hour promise, but Halverson Music's shop owner, Andy Halverson, had brought along his two grandchildren, and the precocious six-year-old boy and four-year-old girl latched onto Adam. He carried them through the nursing homes and the children's ward at the hospital, resting a child on each hip as he coached them with the words to the songs they sang.

Christy's eyes misted when Andy said, "Adam should have kids of his own. He's a natural with them."

Christy agreed with him completely. When Bertha Gonzales invited the entire group back to her house for hot toddies, the kids begged Adam to come. Christy had only to look at his face to know he wanted to go, so they went. The children rode with them to Bertha's house, and Christy smiled to herself as she listened to them fire non-stop questions at Adam. He patiently answered them all, instinctively knowing which ones could be handled by a one-syllable response, and which ones had to be expounded upon.

It was nearly midnight by the time they finally left Bertha's, and Adam was silent during the ride home. Christy sensed that he wasn't upset but introspective, so she didn't encourage conversation.

When they came to a stop in front of his apartment building, he turned toward her, saying, "Thanks for insisting I go tonight. I had a wonderful time."

"Me, too," Christy replied, wanting to say more—wanting to tell him that she wanted to marry him and give him a family as fast as she could. Instead, she hugged him and said, "Merry Christmas, Adam."

"Merry Christmas," he whispered, hugging her back. "Let's get inside before we freeze to death."

They both let out a gasp of surprise when they reached Adam's apartment and the door flew open.

"Dad? What are you doing here? What's wrong?" Adam asked in alarm as he took note of his father's pallor.

"Thank God, you're finally back!" Charles exclaimed. "Christy, your mother called around eight. Your father's in the hospital. He's had a heart attack."

"No," Christy whispered as she stepped back from the door, shaking her head in denial. Her father couldn't have had a heart attack. He'd been perfectly fine when she'd seen him today. "No!"

"He's going to be all right, Christy," Adam said, as he hugged her tightly. She was trembling so much, her teeth were chattering. "What hospital is Robert in?"

"Penrose," Charles answered. "Would you like me to drive you?"

"No, we'll be fine," Adam said as he and Christy headed for the car.

They hit every red light on the way, and each time they did, Adam cursed violently. When he pulled up in front of the hospital, Christy leaped out of the car and raced toward the entrance without waiting for him. By the time he'd parked and hurried inside, Christy was nowhere in sight. He had to ask at the desk where he might find her. The woman directed him to the cardiac unit.

When Adam stepped off the elevator, all he had to do was follow the sound of weeping to find Christy. She was sitting on a low red vinyl sofa, staring helplessly at the wall as she held her sobbing mother in her arms.

"How is he?" Adam asked when he joined them.

"He's unconscious," Christy replied dully. "The nurse said that as soon as there's any change, they'll let us know.

The waiting began. Adam paced, Ilona cried, and Christy held her mother and stared vacantly into space. As the hours passed, Ilona calmed down, but Adam became more and more concerned about Christy. She was so silent and withdrawn.

He tried to get her to drink some coffee, but she refused. He tried to get her to talk, but she ignored him. He sat down beside her and tried to hold her close, but she jerked away from him, which cut him to the bone. He loved her, and she wouldn't let him help her. It was killing him.

When dawn came, Adam stood at the window of the waiting room, watching the sunrise. A bitter smile twisted his lips when he realized it was Christmas Day. Christy had promised that she wouldn't let anything bad happen to ruin the holiday this year. So why was he standing in a hospital facing the worst Christmas he'd ever had to face?

Another hour passed before the doctor entered the waiting room and announced that Robert had regained consciousness and was insisting on seeing Ilona. Ilona left, and Adam turned his attention to Christy.

She looked so forlorn and lost, and he squatted in front of her, but she looked right through him.

"Christy, you have to snap out of this," he told her gently as he took her ice-cold hands in his, relieved when she didn't jerk away from his touch. He began to chafe them. "Come on, honey. Talk to me. You need to talk this out."

"It's my fault," she finally whispered.

"Christy, that's not true, and you know it," Adam stated. "Your father had a heart attack."

"Yes, and it was my fault," she said as she suddenly focused her gaze on him. Adam wished she hadn't, because they were so empty of feeling that it was like looking at two chips of blue ice. "I never should have talked him into working at the mall, but I was thinking of myself. I wanted that job and I used him to get it."

"The doctor said it was okay for Robert to work," Adam reminded.

"Don't patronize me!" she railed as she jerked her hands from his and leaped to her feet. She began to pace in agitation.

"I'm not patronizing you," Adam objected as he stood. "I'm stating the truth. Not only did the doctor tell you it was okay for Robert to work, he encouraged it."

"He said it was okay for Pop to work, but I ran him into the ground," Christy insisted as she stopped pacing and glared at him. "I was exhausted by day's end, so I can only imagine how worn-out he was. I should have realized that. I should have cut our hours. I should have been more sensitive to his needs!"

"Your father is a grown man, Christy. If the job was too much for him, then he should have told you so."

"But he would never do that!" she cried. "He has devoted his entire life to me, and when it was my turn to return that devotion, I let him down. I'll never forgive myself for this. Never!"

She started to cry then, and Adam felt the sting of tears in his own eyes. He went to her, but when he tried to pull her into his arms to comfort her, she swung away from him.

"Don't touch me!" she said shrilly. "If I hadn't been so damned wrapped up in you, I'd have paid more attention to Pop. I would have seen this coming. I could have stopped it."

"Christy, this isn't your fault," Adam stated calmly, rationally—though he was neither calm nor rational inside. It was Christmas Day and history was repeating itself. Christy was turning on him—just as his family had every year—and if anything happened to Robert, she'd end up hating him. His self-protective instincts urged him to leave before he had to face that fate, but his love for her held him in place. "Honey, you once told me not to endow myself with godlike powers. Don't you think it's time you took your own advice?"

Her posture changed, and for a moment, Adam thought he had reached her. But then she turned to look at him, and when he saw the coldness in her eyes, he knew it was over.

Christy confirmed it when she said, "You were right that night, weren't you? You are a jinx, and every time I look at you, I'm reminded of what I've done. Just go away, Adam. Go away and leave me alone."

She turned her back on him, and her rejection was so painful that Adam was sure he was going to die. He wanted to tell her he was sorry, but his hurt ran so deep that he couldn't find his voice, so he turned and walked away.

He was gone when Christy's mother returned to the waiting room and said, "If your father lives through this, I may just kill him myself."

"Why?" Christy asked as a wave of uneasiness swept through her.

"Because the old fool just told me that he'd decided he was feeling so good that he didn't need his blood-pressure medicine, so he hasn't been taking it for weeks!" Ilona explained, furious. "The doctor says we're lucky he hasn't had a stroke, too!"

"Then it wasn't my fault," Christy whispered.

"Good heavens, no!" Ilona said. "You haven't been blaming yourself?"

"I thought it was the job. I thought I'd worked him too hard."

"Christy, you know your father better than that. If the job had gotten to him, he would have said something."

In that instant, Christy realized that what her mother said was true. Her father had never been averse to complaining, and if the job had been too much, he would have told her so. She also realized just what she'd said to Adam. She'd been so frightened and angry with herself that she'd transferred her anger to him. She'd told him he was a jinx. She'd turned on him just as his family had always done. He had to have been shattered!

She ran out into the hallway, even though she knew Adam was long gone. She wanted to find him and tell him she was sorry. She wanted to tell him how much she loved him, and that if he walked out of her life, she wouldn't be able to bear it.

But her father still wasn't out of danger, and she couldn't leave her parents during their time of need. She returned to the waiting room and sat with her mother. This time she cried, and it was her mother who held her; but Christy's tears were as much for the pain she'd caused Adam as they were for her father's crisis.

ADAM CONSIDERED GOING to the mall, but he knew that this time even work wouldn't dull his pain, so he returned to his apartment. It was only when he reached the door that he remembered his father had been there when he and Christy had returned last night. *Why?*

The answer was clear the moment he entered, and he was so stunned that he simply stood in the middle of the room and stared. An American Flyer model train had been set up beneath his tree.

He knew the train was from Christy, because he'd never told anyone else about it, and she must have conspired with his father to assemble it so she could surprise him. Tears blurred his eyes as he walked to the tree and knelt beside the train, gently trailing his fingers over the engine. At that moment, the true meaning of Christmas hit him. It was a time to give of oneself—to love and to forgive; to share and to care. It was, he realized as his eyes drifted to the Nativity scene Christy had given him, a symbol of faith.

All his life he'd longed for one happy Christmas, and though he'd had little control over the event as a child, he could have found happiness in the season as an adult. Instead, he'd sat around dwelling on the past and feeling sorry for himself.

As he looked again at the train, he realized that he'd expected Christy to make the holiday happy for him, when he should have been trying to make it happy for her. Now she was facing her first miserable Christmas, and he had to do something to make it better. He also knew how to do it.

CHRISTY AND HER MOTHER hugged each other in relief when the doctor came into the waiting room and announced that though Robert wasn't completely out of danger, it looked as if he were going to be fine.

"It's a miracle," Ilona murmured when the man left.

"It's the season for miracles," Christy commented, swiping at her tear-filled eyes.

"Yes, it is," Ilona agreed as she smoothed Christy's hair from her face. Then she frowned as she glanced around the room. "Good heavens, where's Adam? It just dawned on me that he hasn't been around for a couple of hours."

"I'm right here, Ilona."

"Adam?" Christy whispered in disbelief as she spun around, sure she'd imagined his voice. But it wasn't her imagination. He was standing in the doorway of the waiting room, and she wanted to throw herself into his arms. But he was regarding her through a screen of lashes that hid his thoughts.

"I'm going to sneak down to the cafeteria for a cup of coffee," Ilona said. "I'll be back shortly."

Christy was too busy trying to figure out how to apologize to Adam to even acknowledge her mother's words.

"How's your father?" he asked.

"Better. The doctor thinks he's going to be all right."

"I'm glad."

"You were right. His heart attack wasn't my fault," Christy continued. "We found out that he stopped taking his blood-pressure medicine. Sometimes Pop isn't very bright. I guess it's sort of a family trait."

"It isn't unique to your family," Adam observed with an understanding smile. Before she could respond, he retrieved the package he'd set out of sight and held it out to her. "I brought you something."

"What is it?" Christy asked as she approached him.

"Open it and find out," Adam answered, his smile widening.

Christy took the huge gift from him and stared into his face, trying to discern what was going through his mind, but his expression was carefully controlled. Uncertain whether that was good or bad, she carried the package to the sofa and sat down. Carefully she unwrapped it, and then frowned in consternation when she encountered a heavily taped box.

"Here, let me get that for you," Adam offered as he materialized at her side with a penknife. He slashed through the tape.

Christy slowly lifted the lid and then let out a gasp of delight when she saw the contents. "It's a skateboard!"

Adam chuckled when she set it on the floor and climbed on top of it. Christy was more woman than he'd ever known, but he adored her childlike qualities. He also knew that they'd always be a part of her, and age would never change that. She was the spirit of Christmas—the embodiment of all the season had to offer.

"I love you, Adam," she murmured as she regarded him with brimming eyes. "I was so mean to you, and I'm sorry. I wouldn't blame you if you never spoke to me again, but if you walk away from me, I'll lay down and die."

"I'm not going to walk away from you," Adam said huskily as he gave her a fierce hug. "Your father would shoot me if I wasn't around to make sure you didn't fall off that skateboard and break your neck."

Christy was so relieved that she could only cling to him, finding reassurance in the warmth of his body, the beating of his heart.

"Why did you buy me the skateboard?" she eventually asked.

Adam rested his cheek against the top of her head and stroked her back. "For the same reason you bought me the train. It was the best gift I could think of to show you how much I love you. By the way, I have another gift for you. It's in my right coat pocket."

Christy immediately pulled away from him and shoved her hand into his pocket, retrieving a palm-size package. This time, she didn't ask what it was, because her heart told her its contents. She impatiently ripped the package open.

"Is it what I think it is?" she asked, losing her nerve when she uncovered the velvet box. If it wasn't an engagement ring, she was going to sit down and cry.

Instead of answering her question, Adam said, "Will you, Christmas Knight, do me the honor of becoming my wife?"

"Yes!" Christy exclaimed as she threw herself into his arms, sending the skateboard flying across the room. "Oh, yes!"

"Then it's what you think it is," Adam responded with a laugh as he swung her around in a circle.

"I love you, Adam Worth," she declared when he dropped her to her feet. "You're my knight in shining armor. My very own special Christmas knight. And I promise you'll never be sorry you married me. I'm going to be the best wife that ever came down the pike."

"Just be yourself, and I'll be happy," Adam told her as he cupped her face in his hands. "I love you—every adorable inch of you."

"Adam, I keep telling you that women aren't adorable!" Christy protested.

"My woman is, and she always will be," he insisted as he settled his lips over hers. Christy decided that as long as he continued to kiss her like this, she'd gladly be adorable.

Epilogue

"ADAM, WHAT ARE YOU doing?" Christy asked with a laugh when he stumbled through the back door, his arms so full of packages that she couldn't see his face.

"The toy store got a new shipment today," he told her as he dropped his load on the kitchen table and pulled her into his arms. He rubbed her swollen abdomen. "How's Mama and Baby?"

"Fine," she answered. It was two weeks before Christmas, and the doctor was predicting a New Year's bundle of joy.

"Want to see what I bought for the baby?"

Adam didn't wait for her response, and Christy gave an indulgent shake of her head. Every day he hauled in more toys to stow beneath the tree, and it was getting to the point where the packages were beginning to take over the living room. But she wasn't complaining. Adam had the Christmas spirit, and that in itself was a miracle.

"You bought a football for a baby?" she questioned in disbelief.

"He'll grow into it."

"What if it's a she?"

"Then she'll grow into it," he replied. "They have powder-puff football, you know."

"What if he or she doesn't like football?"

"You're right. Maybe I'd better get a tennis racquet, just to be on the safe side."

Christy laughed and hugged him. "You're worse than Pop ever was. This kid is going to be spoiled rotten."

On Christmas Eve morning, Christy awoke, stretched, and then widened her eyes in surprise. "Adam?" she whispered, shaking his shoulder.

"Uh-huh," he murmured sleepily, automatically reaching for her.

"Adam, wake up!" she said more loudly.

"What's the matter?" he asked, peering up at her through one half-open eye."

"I think the baby's coming."

"The baby!" he gasped, bolting up beside her. "But you aren't due for another week!"

"Well, the baby's decided not to wait. My water just broke."

"Oh, my God!" he roared, leaping out of bed and grabbing the packed suitcase that stood beside it. "Come on, let's go!"

She grinned at him. "Don't you think you should get dressed first?"

He glanced down at his naked body and blushed from the tips of his toes to the top of his head. "That might be prudent."

At one minute after midnight on Christmas Day, Christy delivered their daughter, Joy Faith, who met her grandparents only minutes later. Robert, who'd spent the day in the children's ward two floors below, was still dressed in his Santa suit, and as he, Ilona, Adam and Christy looked adoringly into the baby's face, Adam would have sworn he heard a distant voice cry, "Merry Christmas to all, and to all, a good night!"

LOVE AND LAUGHTER

Look for:

Delightful, entertaining, steamy romps. All you expect from Harlequin Temptation—and humor, too!

SLIP BETWEEN THE COVERS...

NEW-1

HARLEQUIN *Temptation*

Rebels & Rogues

All men are not created equal. Some are rough around the edges. Tough-minded but tenderhearted. Incredibly sexy. The tempting fulfillment of every woman's fantasy.

When it's time to fight for what they believe in, to win that special woman, our Rebels and Rogues are heroes at heart.

Josh: He swore never to play the hero . . . unless the price was right.

THE PRIVATE EYE by Jayne Ann Krentz. Temptation #377, January 1992.

Matt: A hard man to forget . . . and an even harder man not to love.

THE HOOD by Carin Rafferty. Temptation #381, February 1992.

At Temptation, 1992 is the Year of Rebels and Rogues. Look for twelve exciting stories about bold and courageous men, one each month. Don't miss upcoming books from your favorite authors, including Candace Schuler, JoAnn Ross and Janice Kaiser.

Available wherever Harlequin books are sold. RR-1

HISTORICAL

CHRISTMAS

STORIES · 1991

Bring back heartwarming memories of Christmas past,
with Historical Christmas Stories 1991, a collection of
romantic stories by three popular authors:

Christmas Yet To Come
by Lynda Trent

A Season of Joy
by Caryn Cameron

Fortune's Gift
by DeLoras Scott

A perfect Christmas gift!

Don't miss these heartwarming stories, available in December at your favorite
retail outlet. Or order your copy now by sending your name, address, zip or
postal code, along with a check or money order for $4.99 (please do not send
cash), plus 75¢ postage and handling ($1.00 in Canada), payable to Harlequin
Books to:

In the U.S.

3010 Walden Ave.
P.O. Box 1396
Buffalo, NY 14269-1396

In Canada

P.O. Box 609
Fort Erie, Ontario
L2A 5X3

Please specify book title with your order.
Canadian residents add applicable federal and provincial taxes.

XM-91-2

Take 4 bestselling love stories FREE

Plus get a FREE surprise gift!

Special Limited-time Offer

Mail to Harlequin Reader Service®

In the U.S.	In Canada
3010 Walden Avenue	P.O. Box 609
P.O. Box 1867	Fort Erie, Ontario
Buffalo, N.Y. 14269-1867	L2A 5X3

YES! Please send me 4 free Harlequin Temptation® novels and my free surprise gift. Then send me 4 brand-new novels every month, and bill me at the low price of $2.69* each—a savings of 30¢ apiece off cover prices. There are no shipping, handling or other hidden costs. I understand that accepting the books and gift places me under no obligation ever to buy any books. I can always return a shipment and cancel at any time. Even if I never buy another book from Harlequin, the 4 free books and the surprise gift are mine to keep forever.

*Offer slightly different in Canada—$2.69 per book plus 49¢ per shipment for delivery. Canadian residents add applicable federal and provincial sales tax. Sales tax applicable in N.Y.

142 BPA ADL4   342 BPA ADMJ

Name _____ (PLEASE PRINT)

Address _____ Apt. No. _____

City _____ State/Prov. _____ Zip/Postal Code _____

This offer is limited to one order per household and not valid to present Harlequin Temptation® subscribers.
Terms and prices are subject to change.

TEMP-91   © 1990 Harlequin Enterprises Limited

my VALENTINE 1992

Celebrate the most romantic day of the year with
MY VALENTINE 1992—a sexy new collection of four
romantic stories written by our famous Temptation
authors:

> GINA WILKINS
> KRISTINE ROLOFSON
> JOANN ROSS
> VICKI LEWIS THOMPSON

My Valentine 1992—an exquisite escape into a romantic
and sensuous world.

Don't miss these sexy stories, available in February at your favorite retail outlet. Or order your
copy now by sending your name, address, zip or postal code, along with a check or money
order for $4.99 (please do not send cash) plus 75¢ postage and handling ($1.00 in Canada),
payable to Harlequin Books to:

In the U.S.

3010 Walden Avenue
P.O. Box 1396
Buffalo, NY 14269-1396

In Canada

P.O. Box 609
Fort Erie, Ontario
L2A 5X3

Please specify book title with your order.
Canadian residents add applicable federal and provincial taxes.

 Harlequin Books

VAL-92-R